DIARY OF A DJINN

ALSO BY GINI ALHADEFF

The Sun at Midday

DIARY

OF A

DJINN

Gini Alhadeff

PANTHEON BOOKS, NEW YORK

Pantheon Books and colophon are registered trademarks
of Random House, Inc.

Library of Congress Cataloging-in-Publication Data
Alhadeff, Gini.
Diary of a djinn / Gini Alhadeff.
p.   cm.
ISBN 0-375-40234-9
1. Young women—Fiction. 2. Milan (Italy)—Fiction.
3. New York (N.Y.)—Fiction. 4. Fashion designers—Fiction.
5. Art dealers—Fiction.   I. Title.
PS3601.L365 D53 2003
813'.6—dc21   2002027054

www.pantheonbooks.com

Book design by M. Kristen Bearse

Printed in the United States of America
First Edition
2   4   6   8   9   7   5   3   1

For Nora and Carlo

"I always willingly acknowledge my own self as the principal cause of every good or of every evil which may befall me; therefore I have always found myself capable of being my own pupil, and ready to love my teacher."

— GIACOMO CASANOVA, *Memoirs*

ONE

UNDRESSING

A djinn skips from body to body and dies for none. The body is to a djinn its human bottle when it accepts for a time the limit of one person and one life. A spirit is locked in one for the precise purpose of undoing its knots—all the deviations on the path of blood or breath and the impulse of nerves. I wake up and come to life within its humid membranes, the palpitation of cells.

Talking about "myself" is like peering endlessly into a handful of air. If I stare long enough I begin to see shapes and what I see as I see it and put it into words is as indisputable as a current—you could say it should have gone to the right or to the left, should have been warmer or cooler, but none could have stopped it from blowing altogether.

Past and future tug me backwards and forwards trying to take over whatever room "I," that is the present, may occupy. But the present is the only piece of ground on which one is permitted to stand, the air around a body and in it.

O ne of the little-known sights of Milan, of its *chic*, was a hippopotamus that was kept in its diminutive zoo in the center of town, steps away from the arch that heralds the way to Via Manzoni which leads straight to the Hotel Milan once the house where Verdi composed several operas, down further to Piazza della Scala and just before reaching it on the left was the bookstore where I bought the newspapers and foreign books that alone made me feel the city had not yet swallowed me whole and I would never emerge to make myself known in any other part of the world. A corner of my coat was recalcitrantly exposed, begging for attention, hoping to be caught in a wild current and borne to a land far from this low-lying swampland. For we, my families, had lived a vagabond life, series of lives, from Spain to Turkey, Rhodes and Egypt only to end up in this pit at the foot of mountains that gathered all the fog of the region, a city saved by the electric light and where most people become very pragmatic because the lack of light and nature makes them suppose that all that happens rests on their shoulders. They worked hard, went to sleep early, counted their earnings, as the government took greater and greater shares of it in taxes and health insurance of which they would never receive the benefits. That the Milanese were ordinary human beings was proved by the fact that when they returned from their summer holiday in August, their faces were filled out, for a fortnight they smiled and looked as though they looked forward to the day ahead and took pleasure in rubbing shoulders with their fellow beings. Then it stopped: their light was turned off and they returned to principles of duty and human decency but instinct was forgotten between layers of efficiency and striving and good sense and you couldn't help but become fond of so much withstanding withstood without complaint, the stoic good humor, the brave grimness of it. Shopkeepers never fawned or smiled but their greeting when after several years they began to take you as one of the regulars of the city made you feel more of an insider than any other. The hippopotamus was such an insider: he breathed the city's smog every day and he had learned to eat *rosette,* Milan's crusty buns that are divided into sections around a central one. He stood by the railing of his meager open-air paddock with his mouth wide open and waited for the dry *rosette* to be thrown into his mouth but he did not chew them immediately: he waited for several to be deposited before bringing up his massive lower jaw to his upper in a single chewing motion then let it drop again and one saw with amazement that the dozen or so buns had been flattened into a white paste that stuck to the surface of his tongue. His hunger was unsatisfiable as, one felt, was his nostalgia. I went to him to have a sense of kinship with another exotic—we came from much the same part of the world since I was born in Egypt—yet we had both become pale renditions of what we might have been. He must have yearned for nature—his very hide seemed slackened and puffy from the lack of oxygen. I didn't know what I yearned for, only that I was in a perennial state of yearning. I was very ignorant then of the simplest fundamental things: it never struck me till much later, when I had left Milan, that I suffered from a lack of light, the obscurity of myself to myself.

Yet in Milan I felt very much a foreigner because there the first questions always asked were "Where are you from? Are you American? Your name is not Italian." And they were not wrong because my explanation when I still felt it was my duty to provide one was always long and contrived and I never felt that I had done the question justice. I was always caught between the need to answer and so to respect the curiosity of the person asking and not tasking his or her limit of endurance and interest for what might after all have been a fleeting curiosity.

Whenever I could, I headed straight for my uncle's penthouse apartment on Corso Monforte and there I was sure of the welcome I would receive from Wally which in Italian was pronounced "Valli." She was a lively blonde and had she had an education she would have run a corporation or a country or done anything she set her mind to. As it was, she infused the role of housekeeper with every extra her ingenious disposition could muster: diplomatic abilities, imagination, grace. She had a family but one felt it belonged to some other less enchanted area of her life in which she kept one foot firmly planted when it came to their economic and daily needs.

Wally was my first taste of the Milanese and they were magicians at making you forget just how deprived the city was and how deprived you were if you lived there. They convinced you that it was an easy life conducted among a few blocks, their elegant courtyards with a palm or a magnolia growing happily in them. And there would be a *porti-*

naia who knew you and everything about the person you had come to visit and it felt as though you never left home but simply wandered from drawing room to drawing room in the same house. In the old-fashioned Otis elevator, you opened the iron grill, then the glass doors, and within the smell of recently polished brass railings and leather-covered seats was fragrant. The smell inside those elevators was the smell of Milan. Or rather, the smell of the damp earth of the courtyard compounded by that of brass polish and old leather with that of the oiled machinery of the elevator was Milan to me.

Every city has a mien in relation to the previous city one has been in. Coming from boarding school, Milan seemed to me a city of freedoms and infinite possibilities. Paris from Milan was paradise while when I came to it from New York, it appeared austere. London seemed friendly coming from Paris, small coming from New York. Coming from Milan, any city seemed blessed with particular grace, I mean from a physical point of view as Milan had little to recommend it that way. Its architectural attractions might have been many but somehow one became inured to the man-made and it never caught one unawares as a strain of sweetness in the air or a chilly gust of wind or a pall and color of light. Milan's greyness washed the eyes and the spirit, put one in a state of desire and resignation, a state of purity: anything that came along after Milan—a not-so-glamorous country town, a hillside, a stretch of cultivated ground—could move one to tears. It was sufficient to arrive in Paris, sit at a café and see people who were clearly not Milanese to feel moved. One felt like an exile in reverse: felt at home feeling the strangeness all around. Leaving Milan, its strict dictate that one belong, that one come from there for generations back, the life contained within its streets, the hours it kept so suited to the Milanese nature, its sobrieties, the range of its culinary consolations so untouched by those of any other country, leaving all that, it was with joy that one embraced the freedoms of other cities. You didn't need to know then that what felt like freedom could later feel like extreme solitude and isolation. But Milan, too, was a city in which it was impossible not to learn solitude. It was not a city meant for an outsider, had no services for them. At lunchtime, in my day, people went home for lunch. I went to a café such as Sant Ambroeus and had three or four of their tiny sandwiches in sweet buns, a cappuccino, sometimes a campari and soda and I would return to work tipsy and light-headed up the staircase of Palazzo Bellini. I remembered the story of the nobleman who was stopped by the police. "Name and address," they asked him rudely and he replied, "Bellini, Palazzo Bellini, Via Bellini." He was a real Milanese as I was not and would never be but for the sake of survival I pretended to be one, used Milanese expressions, spoke with a Milanese accent until the day I met Hare who could not abide it and little by little one correction after another banished every trace of that accent from my speech, every vowel too closed or too open which was a dead giveaway for a Milanese. Still, part of me had become and would always be Milanese.

My first apartment overlooked a courtyard. There were three rooms, and one entered the bathroom from the kitchen and it was the place farthest from the bedroom for to reach it I had to cross my study and the living room into which I never went, though the largest room, because it had no windows and only some beastly furniture I did not like put there by my landlord—large square foam rubber cubes covered in a riotous jungle print in all shades of green. The same cushions lined the back wall of my tiny study, of which one wall was all windows so that brilliant light came in, only I covered them with white cotton spreads. I loved to sit at that table and work. The table was a bamboo table I had bought in New York for a studio apartment that was a sort of underground cage I made much worse by painting it dark brown. This, I was told, would give it a wonderful atmosphere, though it made it into a foul den which at any rate was its natural inclination. Always it reeked of the Italian restaurant on the ground floor—the smell of frying garlic and simmering tomato sauces had embedded itself in the hallways, in the carpeting of the stairs and it is a good thing I wore Mitsouko perfume or I probably would have smelt of it, too. A robber, one summer while I was away, came through a skylight in the bathroom and fell with one foot into the toilet before stealing my television and making a more dignified exit through the front door. I had left a detachment of cockroaches to guard the place but they did not prove a deterrent.

In my first apartment in Milan, I was robbed by gypsies most mysteriously for I simply came home one day to find a gold chain gone and not a single thing out of place, as though nothing had happend. There was a robbery in my second apartment, too, on Piazza Tricolore, just as clean and just as mysterious: I found the front door unlocked and the only valuable things I possessed gone.

Maria came to clean there. She was a tall gaunt woman with straight black hair. She had long black hairs on her legs and when she came would walk straight to the middle of the large room, pause, roll down her stockings after unhooking them from the suspenders and her hairs would bristle audibly with electricity. Sometimes she told me of her husband. She had a funny name for his advances: she said that he came near her and made *"moine,"* which means to talk sweetly or make sweet noises like a purring cat. "What does it matter anyway?" she would conclude, "You wash it, you dry it, and it's good as new." Once there was an earthquake while I was sitting on the floor at Piazza Tricolore and it was the only time in Milan I felt something exciting was really happening to me. There were evenings when I would have gone out with any friend but had already run through my short supply of them. They were usually foreigners who were able to have as loose a life as mine. The Milanese mostly went home for meals, lunch and dinner, and to get them to go out was an undertaking. Their aunt, or their mother, was always waiting for them.

I was quite happy doing translations but all the different members of my family, and there were many of them in Milan at that time, felt I was wasted, alone in a small apartment, when I should have been going out and "meeting people." They worried so much they found me a job, a dream job for anyone but me, and on the very first day, sitting by myself in a cream-colored showroom surrounded by racks of red cashmere dresses, at a cream-colored desk, I knew there was no country that would feel more foreign than this. I consoled myself that the palm at the center of the cobbled courtyard was beautiful.

I walked to work down the long and narrow Corso Monforte observing how the soot had blackened the façades of buildings and thinking I was breathing all that was making them black every day aside from, perhaps, Sunday. They called it *lo smog* in Milan and soon it would be paired up with another enemy bearing an American name, *lo stress*. I got *lo smog* and *lo stress* to a great degree and when I hadn't been on holiday for some time, it became harder and harder to get up in the morning and turn on all my pretty electric lights. Even now on stormy days in New York when the sky is thunderous grey and I turn on the light, it reminds me of Milan. Aside from the hippo, I encountered another exotic in Milan, on more than one foggy night—a Somalian woman wreathed in white veils. With her, too, I felt a kinship.

On the way back from work, I would stop at a record store and buy two or three records a day—a group called Penguin Café Orchestra, Nina Simone, Maria Callas singing Verdi, Bellini, Donizetti, the pianist Benedetti Michelangeli. And I bought books, brought them home and put them on a table face up and they would constitute my gallery of friends.

You may think it a strange choice to have cast her into the world of fashion—she was not a likely candidate. But after three years in a boarding school wearing a scratchy grey uniform, what better training could there be for a young woman than to see "luxury" from the inside and close up? To be able to buy every dress, go to the best hairdressers, stay at elegant hotels, eat in the most fashionable restaurants, travel first class and travel frequently. It was, as I'd hoped, a crash course in luxury and it worked very well. By the end of it, she viewed a large tin of Iranian caviar as just another kind of food. She had become an ascetic of excess: indulging in luxuries may have been part of her duties but she became indifferent to them.

In fact she went from one kind of monastery to another as preparation for the rigors of maintaining and administering the corporation of herself.

Though I started writing late in life, I began to gather information long before. The years spent in fashion were given to research because it was not my chosen occupation. I reviled the women caught up in what to wear—being one myself. I reviled the men caught up in devising things to do to the length of a skirt, the width of shoulders. I had them down as ninnies.

One of the first days I walked into the master's studio, my *Herald Tribune* clutched beneath my elbow, he asked, "What's new?" Meaning what had his hero, Yves Saint Laurent, thought of now, for the latest haute couture show in Paris? I said that a certain Ayatollah Khomeini had taken hold of Iran, but apart from that nothing and meant it to sting. It went over his head by a margin.

It was among my agreements with the master's partner that I would not come to work before eleven, the other being that they would pay me a large salary. Both demands were made in the hope that I would be turned down. At my first lunch at the master's house, in the presence of the partner, the Neapolitan mastiff, and a little pile of shaved truffles curling up at the edges to go with the risotto, the master had said, "I need someone like you." I felt like a rare watch. The mastiff wheezed and whimpered in his sleep. "Tomorrow you can discuss how much," he concluded. I looked at his short straight nose, the exposed nostrils, the blue eyes, unlipped mouth, strong stocky body. I knew that he had few friends, that he liked to eat white food such as chicken and mashed potatoes, that he always dressed in blue—blue sweatshirt and pants—and seemed impervious to fashion's ephemeral revolutions.

Before the formal interview on Via Bellini where the offices were, in the Palazzo Bellini, I found out how much the person making the highest salary there was making, added fifty percent to the monthly sum, and heard myself asking for that in a large room with a fresco of a pointy-nosed dog sniffing the toe escaping from the sandal straps of a shepherdess in a flowing pasty gown. If they said yes, it would be worth it, this tedium of the fashionable reduced to the rags on one's back and having to think again and again how to make them different. If they said no I would have to find something else to do. Stop complaining, too. The partner, a bald teenlike man with a mustache, twirled his cigarette on the point of his fingertips and breathed out smoke with the reply, "No one ever asked me for so much, but fine."

On my way out, walking past the fat-calved centurion poised in front of a laurel bush, a laurel wreath on his chestnut curls, I thought, God, what will I do to deserve such money?

I sat on the other side of the table at which he designed collections. Before each new season I would try to come up

with a set of colors, an inspiration. With the book *Ukiyo-e*
he designed an entire "Japanese" collection. All the jackets
had kimono necklines and the colors were murky or, as
Tanizaki listed them in "In Praise of Shadows," dark blues,
browns, lacquer reds, blacks, pewters. One evening outfit
was modeled on a suit of samurai armor and was built of
tubular cords sewn together and covered in bush-colored
raw silk to be worn over wide-legged black satin pants, also
like a samurai's; I wore the combination once and breathed
as little as possible for the duration of the evening. Another
year, a book on the Amish led to a series of rather unwear-
able and unbearably loud quilt-patterned suede jackets—
red and turquoise, for instance—as visible as targets. Once,
I designed some sweaters and gave him the stash of drawings. He transposed them onto his sticklike figures pre-
drawn for him on sheets printed with his logo, then tore the
drawings in half and placed them in the wastepaper basket
saying, "We don't need these anymore." I retrieved them
and took them home as proof of my significance and so,
inevitably, of my insignificance. From the moment I began
working there, I worried about the recognition I would
never receive as éminence grise of the establishment for I
was as immodest as I was servile. No one would have
guessed that beneath my efficient mercurial ability to get
under the master's skin and divine his every wish and bend
seethed the desire to be anointed official muse, if nothing
more, though traffic was feverish around even that modest
post and I was the last in a line of contenders. So I assisted,
and as I did so, resented. What did he have that I didn't? In
his fame and moment I had been assigned a minor role.

Something told me I had no right to expect more: I

arabesqued the master's line of thinking, feeling what he felt, coming up with more but along lines that were after all his. I might once have wanted to set the record straight: how responsible I had been in the construction of the master's name and empire; how I, too, should have become rich; how mean and false the fashion world was. My indignation concealed ambition. Had the world that embraced him embraced me, I might have embraced it. I was lucky, I told myself, because it is a terrible life to become famous for shuffling fabrics on bodies and doing it well once only wins you the opportunity of doing so again, as in all professions.

To dress an anatomy is to cloak an animal. Arms and legs are awkward objects: any article of clothing must take them into consideration. So far from being empty, the canvas is already full and one nonetheless wishes to add dress to it. *To dress,* as in "to season," "to truss" or "to mask." *Porter* in French also means "to carry." Prêt-à-porter is something ready-to-be-carried almost as an object outside oneself. And so it is. A piece of clothing off a rack is for a standard body, therefore for nobody since no body is standard. There will always be one person somewhere saying: this thing doesn't fit, and whoever designed it is incompetent—the sorts of conversations women might have had with their seamstresses, men with their tailors, in the course of a fitting. The flaws would have been eliminated or reduced, the desire of the wearer tempered by the limit of his or her limbs and girth.

I stood by a fresh new monument at whose feet many laurels were deposited, yet I received none and was annoyed. But is it possible to exploit one who freely gives? Naturally not. I had preceded any exploiters of myself in that I did it first and better, offering, furthermore, no resistance.

When I designed I exploited, too, whatever I could find: the forms of knots and folds of origami for a set of costume jewelry; a series of shoes from a pair on Nijinsky's feet painted by Léon Bakst; three colors combined—sand, periwinkle, and tobacco—from a thirties vignette of a cricket match. I stole because my head felt empty at all times. As I said, I thought I despised fashion and considered it not worthy of an inspiration under whose influence I would even then have wished to dwell more permanently.

And I became obsessed with clothes: I found I had to have certain parts of every new collection. Had to have them to wear, and as proof of my contribution, which I never ceased to question in the privacy of my head. What was I offering? There is nothing concrete about fashion, just illusion after illusion and a bit of more or less well-constructed fabric to support them. I kept all the garments in which I remembered my role: a little remark let fall there that deepened the pleat on a pair of pants, my fingers having lingered here on a houndstooth swatch causing it to be made into a longish jacket. The assistance was unobtrusive: I knew that to be effective I had to be barely there, to suggest as a flurry starting from my chest, travelling into the master's and becoming idea in him.

I inhabited a large empty apartment populated by mirrors and closets, and a black floor I thought would be easy to keep clean. I filled the closets and paraded before the mirrors in my spoils of war. I could try on twenty different outfits before falling upon one that fit that day's body and its inability to see itself for what it was.

When I was not working on collections I was answering interviews in the master's name. I gave my opinion on everything. He liked publicity of all kinds as long as it was favorable and preferred popular magazines that chronicled the social doings of deposed monarchy around the world, and in the summer months printed pictures of Agnelli jumping off yachts naked, or of actresses, princesses, and anchorwomen topless.

On some days I felt so stifled in my office that I would crawl across the large frescoed entrance, tiptoe down the grand staircase hoping not to encounter anyone and make my way to the movie theatre across the street feeling miserably guilty but not enough to stop. During my last year there I had to set three alarm clocks so as to wake up in the morning, but in spite of that I never reached the office before eleven-thirty and every day was spent in a cycle of guilt and boredom with brief spasms of alarm at the thought of being reprimanded. I felt justified in my behavior and reprehensible.

The master and the partner had picturesque fights. The first time it happened I retired to my little office next to the bathroom, where I heard the sound of the toilet being flushed all day long, till the partner came to fetch me saying all was calm again. After a while I got used to their theatrics and just waited for them to stop. The partner would yell at the master, "*Non farti delle seghe,* don't masturbate, no one is going to wear an overcoat that looks like a hot-air balloon and costs as much as a Kawasaki."

The real tension at the time was that the master had

fallen in love with a soccer player then in his twenties. He was affectionate and undemanding. He had very black wavy hair, blue eyes, and a deep horizontal furrow between his eyes, on the bridge of his nose. He was low waisted which made him appear taller than he was. To the master he was perfect. The lover said "beauty free" when he meant "duty free," and "Bergford Goodman" instead of "Berg-dorf Goodman." The master had brought him into the apartment where he lived with the partner, who was in anguish though he was only being physically replaced as the master still wanted his wits at work and at dinner. I arrived at that delicate time. The partner would eventually go and live on his own, in an immense apartment with stuccoed ceilings and moldings that he never furnished, and by then his erotic trips to New York had begun.

It was not the master's skills I was in awe of so much as his and the partner's, especially the latter's, lack of inhibitions when they spoke of sex, the first explicit conversations I heard on the subject. The master himself was modest, even shy. If you believed what he said, he often slept alone, and when not alone, slept. He kept his life of passion to himself, and one knew he was contented.

The partner, who had been so shattered in love, spoke of nothing else, especially at the studio halfway through the morning. He liked the mimicry borrowed from a female friend about a girlfriend whom she had overheard masturbating in the dark: he would tap his index finger between his lips in and out in a blur of rapid movement, making wet smacking noises. He, too, like the master, had a new lover, but one he designated with every word and gesture as a stand-in for the real thing and as a means to recover from it.

The master and the partner had met in Forte dei Marmi on the beach, and soon after the partner moved to Milan. He made the master and himself a fortune because he judged everything, especially business ventures, by their potential to amuse him. When his mother listed her grievances on the telephone he told her that she had better find something more interesting to talk about or he would stop calling. Nothing worried him and if he did not know the answer to something he waited. He dawdled over contracts as prospective partners improved their offer thinking he needed further enticement whereas he was simply not eager for the coercion of a contract. The master had been working for a firm as designer, a position for which he got little money and even less credit. It was the partner who had encouraged him to start on his own. They put together a small line of menswear. Their women friends, a few journalists among them, mainly drawn by the partner's humor and his racy talk of sex—boys, bottoms, tricks, how he had spent the previous evening, the length of their cocks and of his own—tried on the jackets whose supple fabrics in mud colors were unlike any they'd seen.

Those women were ready for a uniform, the very one men had worn since Victorian times, that would free them from the preening constrictions of feminine clothes and free them to hide their body instead of showing it. Jackets were what the master knew how to construct, or rather, deconstruct, because soon he became known for his floppy ones.

He always found in models a flaw that made them unbeautiful. More than anything he hated that they should think of themselves as anything special. If they were considered top models and demanded to be paid more, he made a point of not hiring them for runway shows, just to spite them. The master's grandfather had worked for the theatre in Piacenza grooming cabaret dancers' bodies for their revealing costumes.

There was a charming mood at the studio in the first years. We would stop for long lunches at the restaurant across the street. We had first and second courses and stayed from one till three or three-thirty. We had long summer holidays and long Christmas breaks. There were many national holidays, too, that were later abolished in the years of austerity, the years of the Red Brigades. Bettino Craxi and the Socialists were just coming to power and when they did they approached the Milanese designers for funding and visibility. But the master had no interest in politics and never read the newspaper—Christian Democrats like Amintore Fanfani and Giulio Andreotti, and Communists like Enrico Berlinguer, were one and the same to him. For he was dedicated to fashion, to fame, and to little else. The lover waited for hours at his desk in a room adjoining the master's to go and have dinner with him, often spending his weekends there without complaining. I did, too, and had even less reason.

When the time finally came to go to dinner, the conversation was always about clothes—what had just been designed, and whether a style from a past collection had sold well or not. The master was very sensitive to what made an item popular and designed the next collection keeping that information in mind. He was not high strung and strict in those years. He liked to work, so one had to work as much as he and follow him on meals and holidays or one would be left out of important conversations, and decisions. I had no life outside of my life with the master, his partner and their respective lovers. I felt flattered to be included in their plans but found my voided life perplexing whenever I had the misfortune to take a closer look at it.

No matter how narcissistic one may be the one essential perception that is denied us is of us from the outside by those who are not us. I fell in love with Fritzie as my eyes travelled over his face, lingered on his mouth as it formed words, and rested on a spot beneath his eyes from where they did not dare to stray out of sheer embarrassment. It was a neutral zone where my gaze could rest without seeming unduly inquisitive. Of that first meeting I remember nothing other than the firm resolve to court him and that he mentioned a woman whose name, Ovsannah, gave us the giggles, especially since I questioned its authenticity and he insisted that he had invented neither the woman nor her name.

I became acquainted with Fritzie in his Orientalist alcove of patterned wallpaper, Coromandel screen, Christian icons on mirrored backgrounds, read and reread library of books. He had been a night club singer in New York, a photographer in Rome, a lover all over the world and this knowledge was his charm. He spoke the language of love fluently and it was what kept me keen for years—I dare not confess how many.

In New York, then as now, there seemed to be no men for women. We wondered to each other, "Do you think he is homosexual?" And all the most good-looking men were, though we fantasized otherwise. We convinced ourselves they were not, then a moment later, that they were. There were homosexuals everywhere. In our circle, when they were not married, they were homosexuals. If we were interested in them, they were homosexuals. So it was that for at least a decade these unrequited courtships developed and the terms of the un-agreed-upon contracts were mysterious to us then though the frustrations were clear. We thought: here at last is someone to appreciate me. I shall generalize: homosexuals often commented on one's clothes and makeup, thought of improvements; they checked on one's weight, approved of diets, thought of new ones. But they never touched. And while they never touched women, they touched men enough to keep themselves satisfied as we gradually became dissatisfied, wondering what we were doing wrong—in dress or makeup—that we had not attracted one of them yet, that one of them had not renounced his unconfirmed homosexuality to one evening unexpectedly kiss us on the mouth. So we waited for our hand to be grazed, for the assiduous friendship to become a matter of skin and sheets but it never did. Still, the hope remained alive and, if anything, thrived on disappointment. An evening where nothing as usual happened was followed by another evening of not being touched, of not being told one was loved, of falling asleep on despair and waking up to the thought of another ruse. Well, after all, it was a reenactment, protracted ad infinitum, of every romantic novel ever written, all of which should be banned from the vicinity of impressionable young women. The bones of the plot were always the same. A man and a woman met; they disliked each other at first, or simply took no notice; then through a series of mishaps, adventures, chance encounters, balls, masquerades in the course of which dowager aunts gave their opinion, postilions were sent for, snuff was flicked off lace cuffs, carriages were summoned, they fell in love and towards the last page of the novel avowed their love to each other after which, following a kiss on the lips, the book precipitously ended. Young women, women in general, were taken, took themselves regularly to the brink of this precipice. What optimism made them suppose that beyond that brink happiness lay I don't know but it was indeed the supposition: that once all the obstacles and difficulties of courtship were surmounted, a straight smooth road lay ahead, filled with amorous seas, bliss, progeny, etc.

To woo a homosexual was to have the courtship last forever, to have the suspense become eternal. The subconscious must have been romantic in us to not want to spoil love with marriage, infatuation with love, expectation with fulfillment. We lived on that expectation. Did we simply wish to avoid marriage? Did we unconsciously know it was not for us though we thought we were pursuing it albeit with objects of desire with whom we ran no risk of succeeding?

I sent Fritzie notes, amaryllis, a letter of which I recall writing the first draft on a train on a foggy day going from Varese to Milan, and the twenty-four succeeding ones in my little flat in Milan, overlooking a terrace of Mexican-colored zinnias. It was the story of an ancient Milanese lady, as told by her. She had walked into a store and seen a kindly attendant at the far end of it who nodded to her sweetly. The old woman said, "I nodded back, and again she nodded to me, and I thought, 'How sweet she is.' I walked towards her and she walked towards me. I put my hand out to greet her, but to my surprise, my fingers touched the hard surface of a mirror. I had been waving at a reflection of myself! And I thought to myself, 'How sweet I am!'" Fritzie loved the letter and the story but though he loved me in his own way he did not *love* me.

He went to live in Cannes for a time. On Saturdays I took a train at seven in the morning from Milan and ordered *caffellatte,* which came in a cup the size of a bowl with the fat blue *W* on the side that was the logo of the Wagons-Lits. I sat on the left-hand side of the train and dozed through long dark tunnels until emerging from one the sun would flood my face and the sea would be crashing to shore below the tracks. Then I knew I was almost there. Fritzie came to meet me at the station. I brought up with me the finest cashmere sweaters I could lay my hands on: navy blue and four-ply with a button at the neck, or taupe in the undyed yarn that was the best quality. We were instructed to say that the yarn came from the belly of Tibetan goats. I spoilt Fritzie as much and as often as I could, but always as though it were all normal, probably to convince him that if he were to throw his lot in with mine all these treasures would be his every second of the day. Naturally I did not think I could be sufficient.

I expect that Fritzie had, at any given time, at least one person as enamored of him as I was then, only he thought of it as friendship. These lovers of his never usually admitted to their love because they knew it to be unrequited and so to avoid the pain of rejection, they silently continued to court, spoil, bring offerings at his feet, hoping one day to sway him into love. Sooner or later they tired, saw that all their labors would never amount to anything more than the friendship they already had, and withdrew. Sometimes they withdrew suddenly, as I did when I met Will.

I was to go on holiday with Fritzie. He had found a little house we could rent in Pass Christian, in Mississippi. But just then, it was before Christmas, I met Will and was with him every breathing moment, at least on the telephone. Fritzie was chilly when I told him the news. It was the first time I had let him down. He could not understand how my falling in love could upset all our plans. He did not know how capsized my life had been, could not imagine how strange my behavior to him would be when he next saw me. For all the spoiling and courting now went to Will. But since Fritzie had always thought of me as a friend, now he merely saw me as an unfaithful one who no longer treated him as before. The before had been made sweet by yearning, and every gesture, word, caress, had been weighted with unspoken love. Now that love had changed its course, he was just a friend who had led me a dance for a number of years. Not that I didn't love him anymore but the open-woundedness of it was gone, and with it the urgency that had translated itself into an utter unconditional willingness to please him.

The closest I had come to feeling his touch had been one evening in New York on my way back from the Orient. I was staying in a hotel in Manhattan. I hired a limousine, went to pick him up and we had dinner at the Plaza. I wooed him with the banal ostentation of a prosperous businessman except I wore a long black crêpe dress, open at the back and with long billowy sleeves. When we left our table he put his hand on my back. There were many such missed opportunities: we had holidays in Florida—Fritzie was good at finding inexpensive magical little houses at a moment's notice—and there were afternoons spent listening for his footstep at my door. They were enchanted days and evenings and all the time I prayed and hoped and all those prayers and hopes accumulated at the bottom of my soul like a smoldering pool of melancholy. Men came and went in his life and I at least had the satisfaction of enduring. So it was that he could not see why one man embroiled in my limbs should make any difference to our friendship and the way we had devised of conducting it. But it did. It was what I looked for all my life and every time I thought I found it, till much later, when I did, I gave myself over to it.

What is the difference, for a woman, between a man and a homosexual, between a sexual who likes women and one who likes men? They both want you to do as they say. Straight men want you to do as they say about serious things—how to conduct your life, what to do in it, which friends to see. Unstraight men want you to do as they say about frivolous things—how to conduct your life, what to do in it, which friends to see, but most important, how to be seen, what clothes to be seen in. What body to be in to receive others. They teach you to treat the body as a pet—caress it, satisfy it, keep it groomed so that it may please. As much as possible they want you to tame the spirit within to a monk imbued with the elixirs of the disciplines of beauty: eat little and lightly, exercise, find an elegant man to be with—as long as he's good-looking, and, because they worry about your present and your future, he should have money. He should be able to take care of you so that they won't have to and anyway a pet should have an owner.

I have fallen into the trance of homosexuals again and again. An unattainable man has always attracted me whether I liked it or not because it was a good carbon copy of my flitting father who removed me when I was fifteen to a boarding school in Florence. This condition lasted three years during which men became even more remote: they became an idea. I found I could fall in love with the idea, different ideas, of men. The same idea of different men. In Tokyo I had lived in a house where three men slept every night: my father and my two brothers. It is to have a sense of men as creatures when they sleep in the same house as you: you see the white in the corner of their eye they will have wiped before breakfast; you see them in the underwear they will have changed and rendered invisible beneath a school uniform; you see the folds their curly hair has taken in the night, the pimple, the hair on the chin, the dirty fingernails, the mixed smells of soap, dust, food particles, puberty. The last was the one that as an animal made you understand to stay away, a foreign scent. The scent separated me first from one brother then from the other then I was alone because I had always been separate from my father, a man who loved women, I being a woman who loved men. He had to keep me safe from the charm of his charms, from the spells he knew how to cast on strangers. But I absorbed the spills of charms he proffered to women who came to our house, and those that lingered over him when he came home at night. Even if he had been in the company of my mother, he smelt that secret smell of having been elsewhere with his appetite.

How did I become entangled with homosexuals? To please them was easy: they appreciated the clothes on my back: my "more serious" father did not appear to notice. If I lost two pounds they lavished their praise. If I was decorative they rewarded me by placing me in their drawing room. I was decorative by the time I came out of boarding school: having entered it fat, spectacled, barely able to speak, I exited thin, smoking, well dressed. In Tokyo I had not picked up any style. I probably looked as though I came from a decent family, with pleated skirts and sturdy pajamas, but I did not look good. At the school in Florence I was surrounded by girls who thought of hardly anything other than how they looked: the "Chinese" dormitory every evening reeked of the ammonia smell of one girl's slimming cream; she wandered hot and red, imagining a shedding on the morrow. How to wind their hair around their scalp so that it would be straight by the time it was dry. How to pluck their eyebrows. How to apply false eyelashes. How to, how to.

Through the blurred pink of the coverlet, across the multicolored marble of the floor, I see the brown and yellow ribbons on the cherry parasol of a Chinese sylph standing on the round balcony of a pagoda frescoed on the wall of my dormitory, once one of the villa's ballrooms. My grey locker, tall and narrow, containing a black knit suit with bright-colored zippers (my uniform away from uniforms), the school's scratchy grey pleated flannel dress and starched white pleated collar for outings, and the everyday uniform—grey skirt, grey pullover, blue cotton overall, blue-and-white-knit striped belt.

The mistress on duty comes in, walks to the windows, throws the shutters open, revealing the hills, the light of morning. We have ten minutes to get out of bed. Some stay in bed longer. I get up instantly and walk to the hallway outside the dormitory where there is a long row of sinks against one wall, and above it a strip of mirrors. Nearby, another corridor with toilets and showers. Downstairs, the baths. The mistress stands at the door while we are in the bathtub and we keep our undergarments on in the water, scrubbing beneath them so we will not be tempted by our own nakedness.

On the first day of school, at Poggio Imperiale, the other "new" girl, Alice, was minute, had a pyramid of light auburn hair parted on the side, small hands, fingers wide apart and reddened, nails impeccably manicured—cut short and lacquered in transparent varnish. Everything about her was meticulously polished and simple, fanatically determined as though she were in her nineties and after a lifetime of trial and error had settled on a few simple formulas. She had honey brown eyes, a rounded forehead with a pointed hairline, wide but sparse eyebrows, a little nose and full soft lips.

She washed her hair every day, threw her head down, brushed it till it dried, then threw her head back suddenly so it stood off her jaw on either side. She could open her mouth and from the depths of her lungs deliver a quivering rendition of a communist hymn such as, *"Avanti popolo, alla riscossa, bandiera rossa."* We were drawn to each other instantly. We had French as our language of complicity. Alice came from a little town near Biella called Pollone, over which her family's estate towered and her father owned a factory that manufactured cages for champagne corks.

From a frescoed chamber I saw schooled hedges and white marble busts, one of Marie Caroline of Saxony, foundress of our school. Waiting for the French grammar teacher to appear, we gathered in a circle and chanted, "Pray, pray, keep her away." She had promised an exam but had a car accident on the way to school and didn't return for six months. No one thought of it as anything but a coincidence—our prayer that she stay away and the accident. Her name was Ferraresi and she was deaf. During exams we knew we could talk aloud to pass information, as long as we did not sibilate the *s*'s, for those she could detect. She would pass out the exam paper then bury her face in a book and we took to talking. Every fifteen minutes or so, without lifting her eyes, she banged the desk systematically with her hand and shouted, "Silence!" just in case.

Madame Berteschi was our French literature teacher. She was large, with a long face, a small vermillion mouth, jaw-length straight black hair and was given to emphasis and extremes. She came in, sat, opened her large black handbag, took out a full box of Kleenex, a pen encased in a block of wood a foot long, a giant notebook. She rested her hand on a sheaf of corrected papers. "Marina, your work has greatly improved," she would holler, then pause to let this sink in before continuing triumphantly: "I gave you two minus minus plus." The plus was for the improvement and it was said without a hint of sadism; her grading system was merely blessed with a mathematical range unlike anyone else's. Zero plus plus minus, zero minus minus plus—her assessment of one's abilities was never dogmatic: she would add a plus after a minus or a minus after a plus to balance the blow or the compliment. One was on a fluttering scale to which she held a myriad measures.

But the terrorist of teachers who shook us out of any complacency at being children was Anne von Vebern: scorning Rousseau and his myth of the good savage, she lectured on the natural savagery of children and their spontaneous cruelty which was to be excised by education and rigid dis-cipline. She spat the words as though to expel a nasty taste from her mouth, though it was a beautiful mouth in a face lit by incandescent green eyes. Her coldness was refreshing in the midst of so much routine benevolence.

Relatives sent me French books which were all withheld

by the headmistress and relegated to a drawer of her Empire *secretaire* along with confiscated packets of cigarettes and lighters that were never returned. I learned to smoke at the age of fifteen and it took practice before I could do so without gagging. We smoked in the bathrooms. We chose one and piled in during breaks between classes. We huddled on the floor around the toilet bowl, tipping the ash into it as though it were a giant ashtray. Our eyes watered because they put acid in the closet to put us off smoking in the bathrooms though it only strengthened our resolve. We smoked, coughed, wept, wiped tears off our eyes, shut them tight and kept on talking. When we were caught it was because the deputy mistress, Miss Sorci, which means "rats," decided on an official inquisition. She would bang on the door with the greatest number of shadows of heads behind the glass, patterned like patches of furrowed land seen from a distance, and yell, "Out!" We filed quietly past her as she stood by the swing door to the bathroom, her short legs with ankles puffing like pincushions over the edge of blue pumps, blue-wrapped voluminous arms crossed against a blue-wrapped voluminous chest; pearl necklace, red silk blouse; a white powdery face, scarlet lips compressed with rage, black hair, short and wavy, close to the skull. Once, I was the last to leave and did not notice that there was no one behind me to catch the swinging door, and it swung back onto Miss Rats and I was more punished than the others.

Contraband was our pastime: anything we could smuggle in or out gave us a sense of having evaded the school's rigid rules. Marina, who was from Ravenna and whose father was a shipbuilder, received a salame from home. She had flaxen blond hair but the face of a man with a short sharp chin, thick eyebrows, a nose like those on Roman coins, straight narrow lips. A hoarse voice to go with the rest of it. She kept the salame wrapped in a dishcloth, inside her wooden desk. After a few days its fragrance began to permeate the classroom. One of the mistresses, after dinner in the refectory, decided to investigate the mysterious odor. Marina fled to the classroom, got there first and went to stand by the desk, brandishing a kitchen knife she had used to cut the sausage on the sly and eat pieces of it when no one was watching. The mistress said, "Give me the knife." Marina replied, "Don't come near me or I'll skewer you." The mistress approached; Marina scuttled to the door and fled down the hallway with the mistress in hot pursuit, both of them trying not to slip on the waxed marble floor. The salame was finally confiscated as Marina, much to our woe, did not have it in her to harm a fly.

Some took tennis lessons, others, in little rooms off the stairs to the dormitories, took piano lessons. All took lessons in humiliation and solitude and the freedom that comes with both. I walked around the gallery on the morning of the first day that I awoke to find myself jailed in the grandest Palladian building I had ever been in, surrounded by the most delicately drawn scenery—the famous hills of Tuscany: gentle little hills and rows of dark black-green plumes of cypress, the branches of olive trees like silvery hands open along the gentle plains, villas of which ours was one. I was reading *In Cold Blood* by Truman Capote, my hair was cut short, I was resigned with the complete trusting resignation that comes with a belief that no alternative exists. This was where I was. I looked into the faces of the men and women portrayed in the gallery called the peristyle: they had waxy cheeks, auburn hair, rigid postures that spoke of unforgiving backgrounds and rejected any possibility of a less formal world.

The Egyptian teacher who taught us English saw me promenading thus and was taken aback. I was certain everyone meant well.

I fell off a horse, broke my nose, had little pebbles buried in my cheeks and chin. When I returned to the school refectory at dinner time bandaged, the olive-oil heiress at my table slipped off her chair and fell to the ground in a faint. My face was puffy plains and liquid black lines of pupil, iodine, contusions. "Were you vaccinated against tetanus?" my schoolmates asked. All through the night they recounted tales of people who had contracted it and died of convulsions. They described the first symptoms. Sleeplessly, I waited for the convulsions to begin. My mother came to see me, said, "It's not so bad," and to a friend later, "She is disfigured."

The olive-oil heiress who had fainted had a little waist, round cheeks, round big bosoms, manicured nails, a high curved forehead, hair flipped at the ends. She was learning to be an interpreter: take shorthand, type, speak French, a little English. Whatever time was left over, she dedicated to plucking hairs from her face: she would prop a mirror against the open lid of her desk and regarding herself gravely, pluck away hair after hair, pulling back after each extraction to consider the effect. She kept a mustache, however, and bleached it so it was silky and flaxen.

A few weeks after my accident, the physics professor, who always started lessons saying, "Let's undress the chalk," said, "Now you are recognizable again, Ashkenazy." Ashkenazy was a long-faced creature with blue eyes and very long black hair. Aside from the hair, we did not resemble each other. She was subdued, apologetic, skirting the walls. We had race in common, were living in the same Medici villa near Florence, our school, with secret tunnels leading to the center of town, the hills below ruined by the knowledge of being there, by the desire to be elsewhere, the thought that elsewhere might be better, that here there could only be this incompleteness. We had one large room after another as preparation for a life of small rooms and antechambers.

The "speaking chambers," drawing rooms where we met visitors, had long red velvet settees along frescoed walls, mottled marble floors, tall glass doors to the garden, red brocade drapes. As we sat next to a friend or a relative, the separation between the one who would leave and the one who would continue the rounds within, room to room, corridor to corridor, never crossing the front gate, became an abyss. How bad could it be, one sensed the visitor thinking, to be trapped in such a palace? Outside the gates, statues of two naked male figures stood guard, one bearing a globe on one shoulder, the other with a goose nibbling at its hip.

———

Grazia went home every evening to a nearby town and it was her task, since she was released, to run errands for us— to gather traces of the outside world and bring them to us to cheat us into thinking that our ties to it had not been severed. She was asked to buy sandwiches and newspapers and cigarettes, and when she was caught with the cigarettes she couldn't bring them for a while.

She had a great admiration for Lisa and they were a clique of two. Not to be allowed near them was to be kept away from Eden. They talked of Lisa's boyfriend at the boys' boarding school though mostly between them everything happened in letters as they seldom saw each other. Their love dwelt on the misunderstandings that took place in the course of these correspondences and it kept them both satisfied. Lisa was a beauty in spite of her teeth, which were small, gapped, and sharp like those of a rodent. She was slender, had large high breasts and long legs with thin knees and ankles but full calves and thighs. Her fingers were tapered and curled backwards like a Thai ballerina's. She wore her straight chestnut hair long with bangs. She had green eyes. Oh, and she was very intelligent. But we were all intelligent though among women intelligence is taken for granted whereas beauty is not. We were even more resourceful because we were imprisoned and far from the protection of our parents. One girl, Cina, had trouble keeping up with the rest and at fifteen was still undeveloped. She was slight, had a childish oval face and straight auburn hair. She would shriek at one of us to help her with homework or exams and she became shrill if we ignored her. Grazia, who read two or three daily papers and would not allow the school to curtail what she perceived as her rights, led the pack in its dismissal of Cina from our inside world. Cina was tormented and made fun of. She never became anyone's friend. I was on the brink of being considered an outsider but the fact that I could write five or six compositions in English during an exam in what I imagined to be their voice, and pass them, endeared me to the commando. Besides, I had Alice on my side and she knew Latin better than they did.

Around our second year there, Alice fell in love with a young man she had met on one of our infrequent outings. Luigi was thin, gaunt, with narrow teeth and a sly sense of humor. She wrote his name and surname on notebooks and textbooks and engraved it onto her wooden desk with a ballpoint pen, then added her name to his. We all did that. No sooner had we met someone than we would imagine ourselves married to him and the largest prize connected to the conjecture was to take on his surname. Suddenly, one Saturday, in an old villa on a hill, she saw a cousin for the hundredth time as though for the first, they kissed and she wrote Luigi saying it was all over between them and it took him a year to recover. The cousin was a bit of an oaf—large, kind, with a double-barreled name.

Every time Alice fell in love with a new man, it coincided exactly with the moment of falling out of love with the old one. And never in any of the mornings that she woke up did she fail to get up humming and whistling and throwing her head down to brush her hair and throwing it back in fluffy layers bristling with static. She walked around owning the ground she walked on, her swinging hands dominating the empire of molecules at her fingertips. I stuck to her, knowing I had found a savior, a beacon of brightness and eccentricity in the paltry system of justice, tyrants and victims into which I had the misfortune to be imprisoned.

The assurance of food, clothing, lodging was not only taken for granted but despised for being impersonal and organized. We loved to hate the meals we were served in school and to complain about them, though we ate like popes—pasta for lunch, meat and vegetables, and if we did not like stew or roast chicken, we could order grilled steak. Still, we complained that for what our parents paid the school could afford to feed us better-quality meat. There were apples at one time for lunch, dinner, and tea: one more apple, we said, and we would rebel. Ours were the trivial rebellions of creatures who had everything they needed to survive except freedom. More apples and we rebelled. We sat in front of them without eating them day after day and finally the apples stopped. We survived on these infinitesimal victories, as we lost the war over the territory of ourselves. They had annexed us and now they ruled. We could only refuse to eat. I refused till I ate hardly anything—not the pasta, not the bread, not the meat. Grazia brought me fresh white cheese I would nibble when I felt faint. I felt faint often. My head spun. I was dizzy from lack of food and from all the smoking. I wore short skirts when I went out and had dwindled so in weight that I was called Little Bones. I lived on Benson & Hedges cigarettes, letters from the outside world, and the moment when I would see the revolutionary again, only then people like him were called *contestatori*, "protesters."

I thought hard of how much I loved him, accepted to

have been chosen without admitting that it did not feel like love. He attended communist meetings, so at least there was something for me to admire. And that was enough to feed love—that and his raven hair. He was Alice's cousin so we all went out together: the oaf, the rebel, the Little Bones, and Alice.

I've often wondered about the obsession with fasting (they call it "dieting"), which she suffered from as much as anyone else. Was it an attempt to become ghostly or spirit-like?

One summer in Sicily—the castle of Falconara. Through a tunnel carved in rock I descended to the walled-in garden overlooking the beach. Myrtle and eucalyptus provided shelter from the sun which was bearable only till eleven. Lady A. was under a white canvas sunshade. "For breakfast in Paris," she was saying, "I eat a biscuit like this"—she joined the tips of her thumb and forefinger in a circle—"and have it spread with a veil of margarine. When one lives alone, one eats a great deal to make up for it." She had frozen dinners so as not to cook.

A tall iron gate separated us from the bathers on the public beach. Two girls approached and observed us through the bars. "It's like being at the zoo," said Lady A. "Shall we beg for peanuts?"

At breakfast the next day, amid an array of cakes, cereals, breads, jams and yogurts, the assembly was held spellbound by a new guest who announced that she was on a diet that consisted of swallowing one grain of rice first thing in the morning.

"A grain of rice?" all the guests cried in unison.

"Yes, a grain of rice," she replied with the assurance of one who is trying to convince herself. "The first day one grain, the second day two, the third day three, and so on until you get to eighteen, then you decrease the number of grains—seventeen, sixteen, fifteen, fourteen, etc., down to one, stop for a week and start again from the beginning."

"It works?"

"Absolutely. Starch absorbs fats. Your appetite is diminished. You can lose from six to twelve pounds."

Everyone filed quietly to the kitchen in search of a grain of rice. The Moroccan staff were feasting on our leftovers.

I n school no one discussed how to become themselves.
How to resist pleasing all the people (men) around them.
How to resist needing someone in their life to drain them of
any desire to be themselves and drown them in the desire to
be them. By the time I was twenty I enthusiastically awaited
the day when I, too, would be usurped by a man, put at his
service: I and my forces, diplomacies, realms, aptitudes—in
uniform for the cause of him.

There was much I could offer, except to say no. Unsuit-
able men had only to want me and a magic metamorphosis
would ensue. I put them into a washing, tainting, fluffing of
body and spirit, and when they came out they were better,
brighter—practically ideal. I learned how to speak of them
to others and to myself, magnifying their qualities lest I
be tempted to return them to the store behind my own back.
I caught myself whispering, "No, but he could be more
good-looking" or "He is monotonous" or "I cannot breathe
when I am strangled in his embrace." But those murmured
mutinies would instantly be quelled beneath an onslaught
of salesmanship: a sense of humor was tacked on to a niggardly nature, inches were added to a squattish frame, savoir
faire to awkwardness. If anything, I was the one who needed
improvement. A diet, for instance. The thigh could be mas-
saged into sleekness and if there was nothing to be done
about it then the ideal man was to be commiserated with

for having a bad body next to him. I improved them, then lost no time in signing my name next to theirs. Lost no time in dreaming of marriage. Marriage, marriage, marriage. There is no getting away from the thought of it for a woman and it is hard to separate what is genetic, cultural, or historical from what is doomed, slated, or written. Because the most unbreakable marriage, the only unbreakable marriage, is between a woman and her desire to get married.

To think of marriage, to be married to the thought of marriage, is to be the lonely half of a pair of Siamese twins till the will-you's and I-do's that precede marriage. Poor expectant flesh, waiting, waiting. Better to try than to wait. That is not how I thought, no matter what I say now. I was in it so deep I was always surprised and horrified when things did not turn out well, when they ended abruptly, when I ran away, did not return the phone call, or he did not answer a letter.

The first man I lay next to, for three minutes in an abandoned bathtub in the abandoned shed of Alice's country house in the north of Italy, near Turin, was a sandy-haired medical student I never saw again after that time but thought of for months. A number of us had been playing hide-and-seek through dark deserted rooms.

Years later the revolutionary frightened me half out of my wits by taking me through Florence's narrow winding streets flanked by stone walls on a motorcycle. I could see the cycle skidding straight into the wall, my back crushed, my bones broken, my skull cracked on the pavement, my soul in flight, and the impossibility of imagining where "I" would be after all that. I did not like being kissed by him, his steel-wool black beard and mustache, his large teeth pressed onto my tongue, his nose squashing mine till I had difficulty breathing, but I liked the fact that I was being kissed though I couldn't wait for it to be over so I could have the pleasure of the knowledge of having been kissed without the discomfort. It was an idea of love and submission riddled with questions, chief among them being, why did I not love him? He hung signs, organized demonstrations. It was Florence at the end of the sixties. How could I resist, or rather, why didn't I?

The draughtsman sent me a very small watercolor in an envelope along with the note:

"I think of you, I paint, I swim. Typical."

The image was of a lake, powdery brown mountains descending on it like the wings of a bird. A pilotless wooden plane flew overhead.

The idyll. When he was there, I stayed awake every night while he painted. I read, but he interrupted. I had to stay awake, but only for him. I watched a giant perform his delicate duties: his hand like a flesh-colored boxing glove enveloped the paintbrush.

The tip applied one of the millimetrical gestures that composed each watercolor. His eyebrows judged: only three square inches of paper to limit the risk of error. I thought how lucky I was to be the person near him.

In the bed, in his room, beneath a ceiling of constellations drawn in invisible fluorescent paint you could see only in the dark, I waited for the glove to dictate, to push my head down between the legs of the giant. I looked at the stars, missed the glinting of the blade:

"I never fall in love," he said.

I put it into the past tense. Washed as a stone in the riverbed I waited to be picked up, turned over, examined, kept. Hygiene was the ritual before the sacrifice. It was the unpayable price of admission to him: would there not always be, among the millions of pores, one that had attracted a particle of dirt?

He said: A. left her bra on the floor in the middle of the living room; M. did not cook; H. did not speak French; B. did not play the piano as she claimed she could; L. could only have an orgasm in one way; F. dressed like a nun; P. was ignorant; D. was not dedicated to him. We were lying on a bed that floated high above them. Now I don't know: did I come before or after them? "He had not been lucky," I thought.

In the toilet off the corridor my knees touched the door. I thought: "What more could there be? Will I marry this man? Am I to spend every night guarding him?"

I didn't realize that I presumed to be the last—the eye of the target after years of mistakes. It lasted a fortnight. When he returned from his fortnight by the beach on the coast of Sardinia, we stood close together between two cars in a parking lot with the hot breath of June in our faces.

The end felt like the first day of spring. We drove to Venice and stopped on the way. In the garden of his friend he sat on the grass, I sat on his knees. He said: "You don't dress like a woman who wants to attract." The flaw. He was upholstered in biscuit-colored linen, the trousers flapping like loose sails around his gladiator calves; the tie held in place by a gold pin in the shape of a propeller. He wore one of his one hundred watches. He had veiled the beast in sophistication. I thought, "It's true, I'll buy a transparent light blue dress and wear it."

The man at whose house we stayed, in London, was an erudite court jester. We slept in his study, the biggest room in the house. The unjustness of this was clear but he was eager to let some fresh air into the musty hall of his marriage. She had a limp and hid the food. We went to one Indian restaurant after another. Every night I stayed up like a sentinel while he worked. I thought, "At least if I can perform my duties, he will return," though he was right there in the bed beside me. Every night I took a long bath. Sterilized, night after night, I was the one instrument the surgeon did not use. I remembered the morning I woke up lying on my side, covering his back with my body, my mouth an inch away from his neck, my eyes filled with a blur of hair and skin, my nostrils with the scent of soap tempered by sleep. For all I knew he was the right man.

"To kiss her," he said one day when I had the honor, for having survived him, of receiving his confidences, "is like putting one's head in a sewer." From a distance I watched a machine being taken apart, piece by piece. This was familiar, it had been nothing personal. Dentists hovered over her open mouth: she was such a good patient they wished she had another set of bad teeth. They eradicated every real tooth and put porcelain in the front, gold at the back. But the problem was, he did not want her perfect mouth with its memory of putrefaction. And every flaw in every woman was the point where putrefaction set in. Why even begin?

When Agnes arrived in Milan, there were whisperings along the frescoed hallways of Palazzo Bellini: "What was she wearing now?" She was the correspondent from *Fashion Daily* in Paris and she had a pretty curved figure with a narrow waist, shapely legs and breasts, and a beautiful face with pointed chin, blue eyes and dark hair. She wore pieces of fabric pinned in the shape of a bustier or a skirt and always there were enormous bows on her head. We met in Como at Villa d'Este and she invited me to spend the following weekend with her in Paris, which I did.

At her apartment the clothes hung on hooks on the walls and there were hats everywhere. For a dinner she would festoon the walls and furniture with paper and bows. I slept on a "rat bed," which was a narrow folding camp bed. Even when she moved to a larger apartment with her Dutch friend who was part black since he had an ancestor from Suriname, I slept on the rat bed in the living room. In their room, over the bed she hung their clothes to dry on a line and we called it Little Naples. One evening when we were getting ready to go out to dinner and I had been in the bathroom, I emerged to find the door from the bedroom to the living room shut and it became clear from the sounds I heard that they were making love on an armchair just the other side of the door.

We ate lunch at a restaurant called Le Roi Gourmet on

the Place des Victoires and stayed till it was time for tea. We had *salade frisée* with lobster and an endless flow of Sancerre. Max continued to eat long after we had finished and our plates had been taken away: his need to delight in all that came his way slowed his movements. At the newspaper office where Agnes worked everyone came late in the morning because they went to parties at night about which they had to write so it wasn't all fun. They raided the safe in the office for petty cash since they were all constantly broke and in need of cab fare. One correspondent who arrived from America was found during his first week hiding under a desk from the anxiety of being in a foreign country.

Agnes often lost her keys and anything precious. She was given a sapphire ring by one designer and the very first time she went to the bathroom and took it off to wash her hands, she left it on the sink and regretted it not at all. She thought nothing of cutting up a brand new fur to extract from it a perfect length of flounce to garnish a cloth coat or simply to wear around her neck or pin to the bottom of a skirt or the top of a bustier. The rest of the fur coat she would throw away. I had never met anyone who had so deeply assimilated the notion that nothing belongs to us for very long. At any hotel or house where she stayed, she left bits of clothing and it always turned out that she had left them on purpose without intending to: they were things she had finished with.

One summer, she and Max split up and she came to stay with me in the Ligurian village of Monte Marcello. The villagers would lean out of their windows, eager for a glimpse of her in opaque white stockings and pumps in the August heat heading for the "ocean," as she called it though I tried hard to teach her to say "sea" instead. But she was a Californian that way. Otherwise, like all the best people, she couldn't be pinned down with generalities. On the beach, we spoke of love; she pounded the tips of all five joined fingers into the sand to indicate the act of love. There was no question that she would return to Max, only allowances had to be made in that he loved her and liked men, too, and with them he would have his nightly revels in the small hours between midnight and dawn when he would come home and slip in between the sheets next to her in their narrow cradle bed. There, every morning, she brought a tray with slices of lemon cake she had baked the day before and Lapsang Souchong tea in transparent china cups.

I arrived in Paris one day to find her in the kitchen dressed in black lace with jabot flounces at the wrists rolling pasta for ravioli, the black lace sweeping into the flour. She would never have dreamed of wearing an apron or special clothes to cook in. She, an American, had never owned a pair of jeans. She loved long difficult jobs. Laboriousness kept her in the realm of sanity and so she covered an entire screen with black squiggles or tables in minute gold squares and triangles. Having decided she could never speak French like a Frenchwoman she decided to accentuate her American accent. If she telephoned for a cab, she would say brightly. *"Mow-siooo, jow voodray un taxi ow noomerow sis dow lah Roo Catroo, et low nom c'est Mc Phee. . . . M comme merveilleuse, C comme charmante."*

At the butcher's where she went very often and purchased things unusual for an American—livers and sweetbreads for pâtés and terrines, ground pork, veal, pheasant—she would say, *"Mow-sioo, un powtee lapin s'il voo play."* One rabbit was dragged off the kitchen table and around the house by one of the cats and Agnes demurely retrieved it, tied its paws, stuffed rosemary into its chest and stuck it in the oven. There was not a squeamish cell in her body. They had moved to an apartment that prompted one man to exclaim, "*Ah-haaah*—we've come into some money!" The walls were the color of late-afternoon sunlight, there was a grand piano, a grand hallway, draped couches, potted orchids with wispy grasses growing around them and a veined marble table supported by two heads of rams. Agnes had an entire room for her clothes where they hung on racks and she had a proper full-length mirror.

They had come into some money—Max worked as a designer, Agnes was assistant to a photographer who liked his models so still and bleached as to appear embalmed, and Agnes bore it all for money, and to further her husband's career. At some point they had married simply in Paris and I had been their witness and brought as a present a screen painted with the scene of an elegant turn-of-the-century couple undressing, her corsets and spangled scarves, his suspenders and dark trousers draped over the surface.

They had come into some money and they spent it all, mostly on their friends, with the ease and generosity and lack of guilt that really rich people never seem to have. Sometimes Max "fell off the bandwagon," as Agnes called it, and always they made it up. One time after a falling out, Max told me, he came home to their apartment and it was dark except for an allée between two rows of candles which he followed to the bedroom where he found her undressed between the sheets, waiting for him.

All her female friends were "kitties" and if she was talking to one about another, the other became "the other kitty." To go and have lunch was "to tie on the feedbag," and every sentence was followed by *"n'est-ce pas?"* and because Max was Dutch we had all learned to say *"pot-fodori,"* which I think meant "Shame!" I was known as Nefertiti of Milan for having been born in Egypt and for my black hair, and Agnes was Betty Crocker for her baking abilities.

There is a photograph of Agnes, almost classically attired, which in those days was rare, reclining on a white couch, in white shorts, a white cotton sweater and a sailor collar protruding from it, her hair flung back onto the armrest and holding with one hand the paperback edition of *Zelda,* which she had found lying around.

He fell in love, she fell in love, then things were never the same especially when no child came of their union. They separated and for a time the light they made together dimmed on each without the other.

When she decided to return to America, she opened the front door and let the cats go their way even though for one of them she had given up having dental work so that its broken paw might be mended by a surgeon who had used genuine coral.

My employers were pleased at my friendship with Agnes because she could affect the fortunes of their company.

The partner loved to set one employee against another, and one woman against another even more. He would hire one, then immediately another, to perform the same tasks as the first. The first who had been hired through a maze of flattery, and told that all would be in her hands, that she could reinvent the world if she wished, would feel diminished by the addition and supervision of the new employee.

Enrica was a smothering woman who whipped an atmosphere of such rambunctiousness around her as to make even the most pessimistic believe all was well. She had a large frame, black hair, angular masculine features and ran the sample showroom like a stand in a souk. Any remotely useful person on the fashion scene could come at any hour, order cappuccino, try on clothes, then cart them away free. Children were outfitted, as were modest and immodest journalists, their aunts and mothers—Enrica's talent lay in blanketing them all in benevolent bribery. She kept more than one collection in that basement and used one as bait for the other.

Lella was a svelte woman on the brink of middle age. She had a turned-up nose, mahogany hair cut short and swept up and back. She wore trim suits and redrew her lips slightly outside their natural confines. Her eyebrows were impeccably plucked, her makeup meticulously applied, her manicure maintained: nails cut short, lacquered the color of a creamy shell. She spoke some languages. She was to handle public relations but she had worked previously for another designer and her chief attraction was her ability to tell anecdotes and provide "secret" information regarding her previous employer. The partner loved knowing how his competitor did business. Information gave him a sense of security. He asked me, for instance, whether it was true that Krug was the most expensive champagne. I said yes, and he instantly ordered several cases to have at his apartment. The same happened with Lafite Rothschild wine—of that, too, having ascertained its costliness, he bought great quantities.

When we left the office late, which in the first years I was there was nearly every night, we would go to a restaurant near La Scala called El Toulá. There we would drink chilled vodka and a large tin of Iranian caviar would arrive with steamed potatoes and bread and butter. Whatever we had afterwards—roast bass or grilled sole—was never very interesting by comparison. The caviar period lasted about a year and for that year I drank vodka every evening at ten to muster energy for another few hours. For we had been working all day long, I sitting across the table from the master, making my little suggestions.

One evening the partner came in at about nine as we were working and asked whether we would all like to go to dinner as usual. Then he said his American representative, Aldo, had brought him some paper confetti imbued with a liquid that was meant to give you energy. We gratefully accepted the little round pieces of paper and swallowed them, then I went to the bathroom next to my office to brush my hair and fix my makeup. Suddenly, I swayed and felt like leaning on the sink. The partner knocked on the door. He asked weakly whether I minded if we went to the master's house for dinner—he was feeling more tired than he had realized. I was relieved because I had begun to feel strange.

We walked down the great flight of stairs of the palazzo, the frescoes billowing all around us, holding on to each other slightly. I continued to link arms with them even once we were out on the street. We went down Via Bellini, across Corso Monforte, into the cul-de-sac called Via Santa Marta and up the elevator to the apartment. In the kitchen there was a soup that their cook had prepared. We heated it. The partner put it into a tureen and when he placed it in my hands I realized it would take all my concentration to carry it into the dining room without dropping it. I managed somehow. We sat. Then very gravely I said, "I don't feel so well." It caused an explosion of hilarity that lasted several hours. I diligently ate all the food that was placed in front of me to make the feeling at the pit of my stomach go away—a sort of restless quivering as though an army of little beasts waited there to be fed. I did not feel anxiety or fear, only that terrible gnawing that could only be made better by eating and by laughing. We laughed in a continuous gurgle. The partner's boyfriend came in and muttered sullenly, "I wish I could feel what you are feeling." We kept telling him it felt awful, that he wouldn't like it, but burst out laughing many times in the course of every sentence so he didn't believe us.

The partner got up, saying, "It's very warm in this room," and flung a window open onto the chilly November air.

He sat down, then said, "It's very cold in this room," and went to shut the window. He did that all evening—from the table to the window to the fireplace, back to the window and to the table. The house was sand-colored and there were no objects because objects are telltale and the master preferred an inconspicuous obliteration of anything that might constitute a clue to his identity. To further confuse the issue, he spoke with a strange *r*—either skipping or accentuating it, as certain Milanese families do and nearly all members of the Agnelli family; I don't know whether in their case it was due to a French influence or to affectation but at some point something that begins as affectation may become genetic and vice versa. The master's niece spoke that way, too.

That evening I ate boiled potatoes, slowly, systematically, trusting that they would somehow restore my sanity. At about three in the morning I began to feel better and went home. Through it all, the master may have giggled once or twice, but, ox that he was, it did not have much of an effect on him. Some time later it dawned on us that we had taken LSD.

The master and the partner persuaded a princess to wear their clothes a while before she officially began to work for them. A moralistic journalist was certain that the princess had been paid to wear them and decided to confront the partner. She did so, just inside the door on the day of a fashion show, and the partner lost his temper, gave her a shove and almost pushed her down the grand staircase. The woman was shaken, had to be led away to a quiet room, given a glass of water, and talked out of calling the police. The partner had to be talked out of throttling her.

Whenever anyone attempted to damage or criticize the master, the partner became enraged. The signs were unmistakable: his face reddened, his nostrils flared and he walked backwards and forwards briskly, inhaling deeply on a cigarette. He had no intention of taking criticism from the outside though he was devoted to the sessions the master and he would have with the entire staff present when he insulted the master to his heart's content. "No one would wear those clothes," he would say then, "only a tart, or a fashion victim. Don't get bigheaded: a normal woman doesn't want to look strange. She just wants a plain jacket and a skirt."

Another journalist once dared to criticize a menswear collection. The partner came to see us and railed against the woman, swearing that he would ban her from ever attending another show at Via Bellini. He became so excited at this plan of revenge that he started saying he would ban the press from all shows from then on. Just saying it made him want to do it. I was instructed to send out a press release to announce the blackout. Two days later, a journalist from *Time* magazine called and the partner said he would give them anything, even the new collection. It was a rather dull one, actually, of muted colors and baggy shapes, but by then everything the master did was seen as "genius." The regular fashion press presumed that the master had made a deal with *Time*. One old-timer accosted him in a hallway at the Milan Fair, where the runway shows were being held, and shouted at him, "We whipped you up and whipped you up like a mayonnaise, and this is how you repay us?"

I once saw the list made by a public relations man in

Milan of all the important members of the fashion press: next to each name was a figure indicating what would be spent on a jewel to be given to them at Christmas. One journalist's way of accepting gifts was to have them dropped off at her apartment building so she wouldn't have to acknowledge having received them. The PR man called me up hysterically one day, saying the *New York Times Magazine* correspondent was coming over to see the collection and I should order long-stemmed strawberries dipped in dark chocolate to offer her. I thought him a sycophant and being very judgmental of what I saw as corruption, did no such thing. As it turned out the strawberries were not missed because the woman came with her boyfriend and they were busy necking in between trying on leather blousons.

The master had several assistants—for the women's lines, myself and a woman who had been with him many years. As usual, she was disgruntled when she discovered I had been hired to double up on her job. I did not like her Milanese primness or her eagerness to copy established French designers and tried to make her look silly whenever I could. If my opinion was solicited regarding a staid outfit that she was championing, I would say, "Only a goat would wear it."

Whenever she had a few free minutes, she would phone the drugstore and in a conspiratorial whisper order scented douches. The master's lover would invariably be listening and he would wait for the most public moment—in the course of a formal dinner, for instance—to repeat the conversation he had overheard.

When I first arrived, Aldo was to represent the master in the United States. He kept his hair very short and combed backwards, had a ruddy complexion and thick hands and had early on gone in for the exercise craze. On weekdays he wore the master's deconstructed thin-lapelled suits in all shades of grey to green with matching shirts, and on weekends, short-sleeved Lacoste polo shirts. He wore Polaroid gold-rimmed green-tinted aviator glasses which he constantly readjusted by pinching the sides with his thumb and forefinger. Later he took to wearing contact lenses and this made him widen his eyes as though in horror every other second. He'd heard what my salary was, and because the master and the partner loved to raise me and lower him and the other way around in an endless cycle of dividing and conquering we could only resort to scrambling to get the better of each other.

One day he came into the new store in Milan and kicked me in the ankle with his heavy brown leather shoe. The suddenness of the kick took me by surprise. A few days later it became known that he was HIV positive. His partner, a Mormon, had succumbed to every possible disease brought on by AIDS. He had become a skeleton, lost his eyesight, and died a slow wasting death through which Aldo had tenderly nursed him. When Aldo himself got pneumonia he must have given instructions that he did not want to be kept alive because he died immediately of that first illness—he let it kill him, quickly, quietly, relatively painlessly.

Till they became ill, the partner would travel to New York often, sometimes for a weekend, and stay at their apartment. They would order up men for him and he would spend his days in bed, only leaving to go and visit the baths, the piers, or the discotheques. The partner, too, died of AIDS but by that time I had left the company. He said, when I told him I intended to resign, "I would resign too, I am so bored, but I can't because I am a partner here."

Little by little, I started to pull away from the monastic life of fashion, and as I did so, the master began to guard me closely, to insult me in case I might think of myself so highly as to consider leaving him. The more detached I became, the later I came to the office, the more he watched and insulted me. One day I gave a writer who happened to be friends with another designer an envelope containing a translation. I had done it to break the monotony of fashion. The master was persuaded that I must be selling my designs elsewhere. He forbade me from acknowledging members of my family who worked for, or were, the competition. Spies would report to him and he would reprimand me, "You were seen saying hello to your uncle on the street yesterday."

He put an eagle insignia on the glass door to the offices and it was clear from that time on that we worked for a regime, of perfume, menswear, womenswear, sportswear— and it was only the beginning. The more money there was, the more success, and the more dissatisfied the master seemed to become. He read of other designers in the papers and envied whatever recognition they got. A lot of the exposure had little to do with recognition and everything to do with money. The partner took the fees the master got for designing other companies' collections, gave the master and himself a small stipend and invested the rest in four-to-eight-page ads in fashion magazines. It was a flaunting Milan had not seen before and soon copied. Magazines began to calculate how much advertising a designer had paid for and offered a proportionate amount of editorial space. The trades were sometimes openly discussed.

Two things had broken the spell of my dedication to the master and the cause of his empire: my frequent escapes to Paris, and meeting Will, an American who had been living in Naples and was an actor in an avant-garde theatre company.

The actor scrawled in his journal: "I really didn't like her the first time we met but I figured if Alan liked her so much I'd give her a second try at some point. I think they were having an affair though I had never known Alan to have an affair with a woman before, or maybe just one. I thought she was a snob—real distant. She was in that stupid fashion business I don't give a shit about and she liked books and I don't give a shit about books either except Hemingway and Chandler and some of Shakespeare—I always wanted to play Iago.

"When I came to do *Tango* in Milan, I didn't know anyone in Milan. I never spent much time there. I had forgotten all about her, but I opened my book to see if there was anyone I could call to have them come to the show and I found her name and her number in her handwriting. I called her at work and she said she remembered me and that she had just finished talking to a critic from *Il Messaggero* who told her I was the *astro nascente,* the rising star, of Italian theatre. Great timing—thank you very much, Mr. Critico.

"We met for a drink at Ginrosa on the Piazza San Babila. I was late. Those Milanese do everything early—have lunch when I'm stretching, dinner when I'm rehearsing, breakfast when I'm going to bed. That's why I like living in Naples—I'm always late.

"She was better than the time before. More relaxed. I

could think of nothing but *Tango*. I talked about *Tango* nonstop—the scene where I take all my clothes off in the shower and the water is tubes of blinking green light, to give people a thrill, and the scene where I dance with a vacuum cleaner which was inspired by a dance Fred Astaire does in one film where he dances on the walls and ceiling. I talked about the tour and the Mafia stealing our equipment and having to buy all the scenery and costumes again. I told her about Tonio the director and about the others in the group. I could tell she liked the whole thing. She gave me a list of people to call and said she would tell those she knew about the show and get them to go to the opening-night performance and pay for the tickets because we always need the money.

"The next night I went to her place for dinner and she made tortellini with melted butter and sage and parmesan and salad with the best dressing I've ever had. It was real simple after all that Neapolitan food. I love Neapolitan food but it gets heavy after a while. The only other salad I like is the one they have at Dante e Beatrice on the Piazza Dante in Naples. It's called *cappucchiella*—"cunt hair"— because it's curly and grows wild.

"After dinner, we planned the party for after the show in a disco called Primadonna—the food, the guests, the music. I told her about Angelo a bit, not going into detail or anything, just that he always asked every new man he met, 'Are you normal, or do you go with women, too?' Anyway she knew about fags, they were all sweet friends of Dorothy's as we used to say in California where I come from. I told her about Tonio and how I met him when I was working in Angelo's gallery and how I decided to join his theatre company, studying to be an actor in San Franscisco and all that. It got to be past midnight. Too late to take the train back to Torino. She said I could stay and sleep on the couch. Nothing happened.

"For a week I hardly saw her. By the time I got up in the morning, she'd be gone. Except once we had coffee together. When I got back from doing the show in Torino, she'd be in bed already with the door to her room shut. I noticed sometimes she must have had dinner alone because there was a plate in the sink. I started to think about her on the train to and from Torino. I'd get into my clothes right after the show without even taking a shower so I could catch the earlier train to Milan, hoping she wouldn't be in bed yet by the time I got there. Still the door would be shut.

"I can only drink champagne. I don't like alcohol. My father was an alcoholic. I could become one if I don't watch out. I'd rather not touch the stuff. The night of the opening, the night after the first night I slept with her, we went back to her place. She had a bottle of champagne to celebrate but I practically drank all of it and fell asleep on the floor and she had to drag me to the bedroom and undress me and put me to bed. But I made up for it in the morning.

"The last few months with Angelo, I'd been having an affair with a Neapolitan girl. Real strong body, kind of big. I tied her up. Not real violent or anything. Kind of theatrical. I just liked being with someone my age. Real sweet and innocent but real sex-starved and that was nice. I mean sex with Angelo never did it for me. He could kiss, though. Taught me how. Said Americans kiss one way, and that's it. No imagination. I picked up biting and sucking from him.

Someone said the best lovers are bisexual. I think she said that.

"The day after I slept with her the first time, I called the Neapolitan girl to tell her it was over. I still love her. I still love Angelo. I never stop loving people once I love them. Even if I don't see them anymore I don't stop loving them. They write me letters sometimes. I can't face losing anyone. I still miss the Chinese girl I went out with in high school. My muscles were built up from playing football. My thighs were so big all my pants fit tight. She was this little girl. I could pick her up and turn her around with one hand. It was the best sex I've ever had. Maybe I should have stayed with her. I don't know. She made me so jealous I got over being jealous once and for all. The day I found out she was fucking another guy at the same time as she was fucking me I went into the locker room to find him. I wanted to kill him. I don't remember much, just this rage like I wanted to bust windows. The moment I realized I could kill him I stopped. It cured me of jealousy. Now I don't mind if the lover I'm fucking fucks other people. I like fucking other people, too. An old Neapolitan friend of mine who's been married thirty years says if every day you have spaghetti and one day you have rigatoni, the next day you like your spaghetti even more.

"She was not the kind of thing I notice right away. A good face but unsure of her body. I made love to her on the floor of her apartment and I could tell she was embarrassed."

He wanted to marry her—well, I put a stop to that. Very painful, but it had to be done. I threw a nymphomaniacal actress in his path at a disco in Naples and he fell for the rigatoni right away. Only not just once. He couldn't resist someone who couldn't resist him so many times a day. He told Miss Spaghetti on a ferry one sunny spring afternoon back from a spree in Capri. Or maybe that was the time he asked her to marry him—it doesn't matter, I tried to erase him from her brain because he was poison and as you can see, I nearly succeeded. There was a ghastly interlude in a bleak and narrow hotel room in Brussels. That room might have been designed for the horror of the one night I did not manage to wipe from her memory: it had two single beds lined up by the wall lengthwise and a view of the clock on the façade of the church across a narrow street so that an ominous grey stone wall made up one side of the room. During that night, he slept peacefully on his little cot while she debated whether to continue with him as he so sensibly suggested, while he swung from her to his fiery new lover, or to give him up. The difficulty, having imagined doing without him, his presence, his broken conversation, the solace of his body, was to give up the smell of his skin. But she did: she gave him up. It was the luckiest night of her life. With him she'd been a body through and through. Most times they met she left her brain outside the door, gave it a rest. But that is a trick easily repeated once learned. I persuaded her there was no need for him. She was to wake up each morning, look in the mirror and repeat, as a friend told her she must, "This man is trying to kill me," till she was cured of him, and later, till she came to see it my way— that she'd been one lucky spaghetti.

I almost bought another blue jacket. I stopped halfway through the gesture of diving into its concealing regimented folds. It was double-breasted and long. I have had at least a dozen like it in my life. I had a pair of wool ones that I wore uninterruptedly for three years. My first blue jacket was part of the uniform of the Sacred Heart in Japan. Beneath it was a blue dress and a white blouse. But my two blue wool jackets were a prelude to a decade of black and it was then that the uniform went as far as it could in abolishing not just vanity but the body itself, instrument of vanity.

It began surreptitiously: I started wearing a pair of black pants. They were Turkish harem pants and I wore them under the blue jacket. Then I found another strange pair of pants, made of synthetic stretch fiber and shaped like an hourglass. They were low waisted, wreathed at the waisband, and they opened out on the hips in a fanlike curve that closed in again around the ankles. They were black, too. I grew so fond of them that I set aside the harem pants and wore only these. I had a seamstress make me another pair but though I wore them till they started to come unstitched at the seams, I never liked them as much as the original pair.

The softest blue jacket I ever owned was made of blue crêpe and I wore it so much the silk lining ripped. For years, I simply bought things to go under and with it: there was no question of not wearing it for even a day, until I found its replacement—the same, only in slightly heavier fabric and somewhat shorter. I wore it every day, too, and one day when I tried on the older one, I couldn't understand how I had kept on wearing something that had become so shabby. The blue crêpes have been set aside now but I could never give them or throw them away. I always think of when I will be shapeless and old and how handy it will be to have these rags to cloak my declining body.

A fashion journalist who was once a schoolteacher looked at herself in the mirror and decided since she would never be beautiful that she might as well confection herself as an object not to be touched: hats with lightbulbs going off and on, a wave of grey-black hair cut to wind its way from the hairline to the eyebrows, two wisps to fall over one eye, practically in it—the precision of this renewed and re-created every day by her personal hairdresser.

To enter her house was to be assailed by the smell of a thousand bodies preserved for decades, for the walls hid closets that hid collections of clothes that had once belonged to others and in which they had braved parts of their life. The clothes had been given away when they had become stained, been discarded, or when their owners had died. The smell was a smell of strain and difficult life.

In London, I found a long black crêpe dress with thirty cloth-covered buttons from the neck to the belly button and as many hooks. Its sleeves were of pale yellow crêpe-de-chine with white daisies printed on them. Since it was a dress from the 1800s, it fell to the ankles. It suited my thin torso and hips, and I wore it all the time, day and night. A friend's mother who brought out raw liver on butcher's paper to persuade us to stay home for dinner, asked him whether I had wooden legs that I should always be hiding them. In the streets of Florence men made their hands into scissors as though to cut a piece of my skirt off. But I was happy in my shroud, certain of its beauty, certain that it hid me from view and obscured whatever I had no idea I was, even then.

TWO

THE CASTLE

If even I who am a djinn don't belong to the body I'm in, how could one person belong to another? I chose Hare for her because he was not "free," as humans say. A "married man" was a way, I thought, for her to get used to the idea that people are not possessions. Also, that one must be free to listen to one's djinn, to have one's ears and eyes open. Humans call this to be "independent" but that's idiotic because if you just consider the fact that without air any one of them would die, they are all supremely dependent, addicted even, to each other and to the earth on which they are allowed to exist for a time.

No, I thought—a long relationship played out over short fragments of time. I think she once calculated that she had spent in ten years a total of three months with him, give or take a week or an afternoon here and there.

Some of her friends thought this "very European," or "very sophisticated." They thought it eccentric and charming behavior on her part when in fact she suffered because she was not as clever as all that: or even if she had been, she didn't know it. It took a decade for her to begin to see the real mystery of life: that no one is alone and everyone is alone, as luck and the laws of the universe would have it.

Before she began to appreciate this state of affairs, she had some sulky Sundays and moony Mondays, thinking how different it would be if he had been there. Still the grey squares of the days in a week were lit bright by the knowl-edge that on Saturday she would see him. On that day she would wake up and fly around the room in a dizzy state of glee.

Then, suddenly the Saturdays vanished and he began to appear at a moment's notice, since he lived down the street, on a Monday or a Wednesday or a Tuesday or a Friday. He appeared more often than before, but he came like a sud-den burst of sunshine from which she sometimes had to dive beneath a parasol. For the visits were unexpected and at times so brief as to be counted in minutes. Still, he had a gift for never seeming rushed. He came and sat and they talked and she felt as though every second of every hour of the present, which is infinite, was theirs. And she was always ready to receive him. That was the secret of my strategy— that by living in a way that admitted no speculation, or pro-jection, any plan she made flew out the window if Hare was to enter through it. Any moment of her day or night was his as far as she was concerned and it meant she became very accustomed to not having it be hers, *accustomed to not being accustomed to anything much, other than a night's sleep and regular meals. Now that to a djinn is the begin-ning of some useful knowledge—a total nonchalance as to the way a day chooses to spend itself. So, though at times I might have been moved to soften the edges of the situation, I didn't let up. I made of her a pliable body any djinn would be happy to inhabit—a fearless body.*

It was never women, neither his first wife nor his second, that I felt crowded out by, but by his books. Whenever I went to his house, someone had called it the Gloomy Castle and the name stuck, I could hear them whispering, elbowing each other aside, "Move over," only they were saying it to me. Hare's mother agreed; she said in her girlish voice, "Soon we shall all have to sleep in the entrance." The books came in crates, they came in pairs and by the dozen. At first they filled the many shelves already in the house, then more shelves were built to line every inch of the walls that wasn't taken by a painting. Little Bulgarian folding bookcases began to be posted in the hallways and passages and against windows to contain more books. Books covered every table in tall teetering piles. Books were on a low wooden stool in the small elevator, and the pile rose and rose until someone leant on it and it fell over and Hare would displace the piles into some hidden corner or onto a vast low wooden plank in the large room that under its previous ownership had contained a vast collection of medieval armor—one breastplate had a neat hole in the place of the heart . . . where I was hit when I first caught sight of Hare. "The hare," the artist Joseph Beuys said, "has a connection to birth. For me the hare is a symbol of incarnation."

Hare would come in the afternoon, I would give him tea,

and we would go to bed and sleep afterwards in a cloud of peace. If everything and everyone becomes family, where does one breathe? I could accept the most that love had to offer and leave the crumbs of marriage to those with birds' appetites. But then what did I know of marriage?

I have always found imperious people restful, their certainties regarding what ought to be done, or what others should do, a welcome respite from the misguided notion governing most of our lives that one has a choice. For to enter life is to come to grips with imperiousness itself—an iron hand that propels one inexorably to extinction.

It is a good thing I am like that, or I am like that because I had a childhood as seamlessly managed as a five-star hotel, every decision taken by a relay of aunts, grandmothers, nannies overseen by the Éminence Grise Himself, my father. To be in doubt was, I think, considered a paltry circumstance left to creatures of less fiber than it was presumed we had. What a mixed time and geography I inhabited—the Levantine woman's imperative that no man should ever be neglected, which was the nature of life in Alexandria where I was born, was later reinforced, from the age of ten, by a five-year stay in Japan, though tempered by my father's quickness to grasp that a woman could have a different life. That she might get an education. Choose a profession for herself. Be independent.

He did not approve of fashion. He gave me money to have a year or two to think what to do next. What I did right away was to escape from Milan. That he had made it possible did not mean it pleased him.

I escaped and went to live in a friend's guest room in New York—on the street where Hare also lived and where I met him, since we met at his house. He came to visit me and sometimes we would drink tequila out of two small glasses I kept on the mantelshelf. There was a grey corduroy couch that turned into a raftlike bed we called the swimming pool because of its raised border. All around were piles of paper. There, too, my father came and said, take an apartment, you can afford to, this is no way to live. He could afford to, it turned out, and for a time sent me enough to cover the rent of my folly and his disguised as the sensible way for a young woman to live. When the money he had set aside for me ran out, I had no idea how to come up with the amount required of me each month. I was living so beyond my means, I might as well have been an addict. Hare, too, had said, "Take it," when he had seen the apartment with me. The price did not faze him. I was the only one fazed, but his and my father's lack of dismay calmed my fears. I presumed they must be more responsible than I, more sensible, and if they thought nothing of that rent, who was I to be afraid of it? I think my father saw it as a trampoline into a finer world where somehow money would be no object, if not immediately then at least a year, or two, or three down the line. The last thing I expected was that I would have to pay for it single-handedly. It was the predicament that proved to be the perfect long-term solution to all my financial worries: or rather, how to become an usher to money and never worry about it at all, other than to accept any gainful employment offered.

Practically the moment I moved into the apartment on Sixty-third Street I began looking for another: my life in that ideal of houses was plagued by frantic searches characterized by an initial gloom and resistance at the notion of the disruption ahead, then by a fixation with the problem sometimes followed by an infatuation with one or another apartment, and the realization of the financial aspect of the enterprise followed by procrastination, then postponement and a sense of relief.

I bought two tables, all the furniture I had for a time. The very first day I set out, I found the first—a narrow rectangular table with fat legs—and if I pulled on the ends it multiplied itself to five times its original length; the second was an oval table that could wind up or down to the desired height. I moved it by the window and that is where we ate when Hare came, overlooking the terrace and the tree. A friend and neighbor immediately told me the tree would never look different from the way it looked now, in mid-February: dry and dead. But he was wrong and the tree became one of my greatest consolations. Its branches were covered in seedpods that sprouted in June and dried and shriveled the rest of the year so that when the wind blew, the rustling of the seedpods made a whispery sound. I never felt alone in my treehouse, thanks to the whispery tree, but I always felt poor in it. The rent rose, then fell after I made some entreaties to the landlady whose mother had died, then rose again with the coming of a new owner, a physician, parachutist, motorcycle rider, father of two, married to a pediatrican, who announced to me on our first meeting, at which he also explained how turbulence is caused, that he intended to end his days in the building. He asked me to make a list of the things that might need to be fixed so that he might do so a little at a time and I did not have the heart to tell him that a man who had previously inhabited his part of the house had jumped out of the window and his wife had found him down on the pavement of their little garden. I also didn't say, believing it to be obvious and hoping he would know, that what mattered to me most was that the rent did not go up. It was a misunderstanding from the first as our first meeting consisted of his kindness hoping for a higher rent and mine hoping for a lower one. After an exchange of letters made our cross-purposes clear, our dealings became more open.

How did I land in a circumstance that by degrees revealed itself to be intractable? I had no idea what I was getting into. I became stuck on the substance of a house and like any addict found I was in no position to support my habit. Before the apartment, I would look down my nose at most assignments offered to me—a famous hairdresser in New York, an elegant dealer of antiques in Paris— and turned them down. At the time I considered my writing hands as pure and delicate flowers wrapped in kid, only to be unwrapped on special occasions. I had not yet understood that the subject was irrelevant if only one was in the mood to write. "Why shouldn't man," said the philosopher Wittgenstein, "consider his own name sacred? It is after all the most important instrument he has been given, and on the other hand it is an ornament which is hung around his neck at birth."

I turned down much of the work that came my way and waited for the ideal which became a sickly mirage—a combination of the little I knew and the vast amount I didn't. Until I moved to my beautiful apartment.

Every now and then, I resumed my search. I found one apartment on Sixtieth Street that was two rooms overlooking the backs of brownstones and their gardens and had a huge fireplace. Hare came and said, "You will never see the sun here." A friend decreed, "The building is in a terrible state." Having made an offer that was accepted, I promptly withdrew it and with a sigh of relief relapsed into my customary monthly frights as to how I would assemble the necessary large sum that I felt would be a great deal even if I had had to pay it just once instead of twelve times a year. But on that sum the charmed nature of my daily existence depended—to work in a square white room looking at the little door onto the terrace and tree—wisteria in spring, roses in summer and fall.

The spell that that one tree cast made a prisoner of me. And though I recognized as the years went by that the hardship of meeting the payments had also made me into a hardworking writer, I still could not resist the temptation to "solve" my problem. Another apartment had a bedroom overlooking a magnolia that flowered in spring which was when I saw it in tenderest pink bloom. There was a strange warren of corridors and some steps leading up to the main room and I never took to the kitchen with a window offering a bleak view of the wall of a tall building but I liked the long room well enough and thought of ways to make it more square, like the one I was in. Hare came and said, "I cannot say I like long rectangular rooms with windows all at one end." I had made an offer to the owner who was in Singapore or Hong Kong and he was very pleased to be receiving one when once again I withdrew it and fell back into my impossibly perfect apartment and its dizzy rent. (Some time later, the magnolia was cut down and a tall building went up in that little garden blocking the light.)

I realized that the solution would be to look for a smaller place. I mentioned this to a real estate agent who rented the apartment below mine, and to my dismay she found something for me to look at right away.

It had a square room, this time overlooking a lovely street of brownstones, a very small bedroom with a barred window, a kitchen in the passage between the entrance and the main room, a terrace with a view of the prettier side of the city and of the park. It was inexpensive, and punctually I made an offer. This time, when the owner countered through the real estate agent with a figure only risibly higher than the one I had stated, I made no further comment and though the agent urged me tactfully several times, even going so far as to say that the owner was negotiating but really did not like the prospective buyer and would much prefer me, I remained silent. I could not utter the necessary words that would further the process of leaving my constricting paradise. I reasoned and reasoning brought clarity as to the utter perfection of the little apartment. The more I thought about it, the more perfect it seemed, in spite of its drawbacks. I knew I could be happy there. Or better yet, I knew it wouldn't matter at all because in this later phase I had begun to realize that I could spend entire afternoons with my nose stuck in my work, my eyes flitting from the screen to the keyboard. I would look back over a year and be pleased at all I had achieved in the course of simply attempting to pay the rent. But the temptation to solve my problem resurfaced.

This time I was able to do almost nothing about it. It was as though my body rebelled. I asked to see what apartments might be available, listened to descriptions, then did not ask to go see them. I took a sort of listless interest and after a day or two, no interest at all. I could no longer throw myself with energy into the possibility of making my life easier for myself. For somewhere deep within me, I knew I had met my intractable problem face to face. What was the real reason that I continued to live where I lived? There was no reason except that I did so. And then it came to me: what confused me was the notion that the ideal solution was there within my reach when in fact it was not. There is one set of circumstances—one's very own that could never be anyone else's, which is why this is so hard to understand and to *accept*—that can loosely be described as one's fate. By it, an entire life takes shape and one person becomes distinguishable from the next. The temptation to change that set of circumstances for a supposedly more practical one is to be resisted at all costs. And so, like Hare, who was the "wrong" man for me because he was married and could not have children with me, the apartment I could not afford was as perfect for me as he was. Hare's absence made me whole, and the absence of money which my apartment constantly renewed removed an infinite range of distractions and "choices" from my range.

And every day, as I went about making a living to be regularly frittered on rent, I drew further away from an image of myself as anyone knowing anything but a detail of what might prove to be my existence. I moved out of the part of myself that willed being in one place as opposed to another.

I threw away, gave away, tidied possessions. I went through every box, pile, and hidden corner of every closet, shelf. I sifted through the sheafs of paper that had accumulated all around my computer for the past decade and all to have two neat rooms with enough space in the closets to put my dwindled belongings into.

The sun was going down. I saw a corner of the park and many terraces, most of them with lovely big potted trees on them and vines and flowering bushes. Here, in my new treehouse, I go from studio to bedroom to bath to kitchen in an elliptical motion. This is my laboratory. I am a djinn in her bottle, looking up at the sky.

Hare could more easily come to live with me in my six hundred and fifty square feet than I with him on his five floors. The reason is simple: there is more room here.

I saw her walking down the opposite side of the road in what appeared to be a yellowish wind jacket and large sunglasses. I knew who she was right away. Did she know who I was? She walked down the street she had once lived on, furtively looking right and left as I did, since knowing that she had arrived. I peered at the house at regular intervals from my window, thinking it would yield some information of differentness. Didn't it know who was in it? One could learn impassivity, equanimity from a house, from any object, from matter. Whether Hare's house had me in it or her, it looked out and in at the world in the same impassive way. The castle, as we called it, didn't mind having twenty-five wives in it or none at all. I looked at it: the same brown-maroon façade, the water stains beneath the windows, the piece of stone of a different color beneath the roof. The windows stared out unseeingly—the eyes of the house appeared to say, "Do whatever you wish, I take no notice."

Out of the top of the house, the two ginkgo trees in Hare's backyard emerged suddenly green at the start of spring. A piece of black plastic trash bag had become caught in the branches and was being progressively obscured by the bright green of the leaves.

I relegated myself to my own world, the one separate from Hare, a strangely old-fashioned one like a model without the improvements, the me before him. I know nothing of families. I may die knowing nothing of families or they of me. Only happiness comes over me sometimes with unbearable intensity: it feels natural the way unhappiness never does. And the happiness, too, is free to come and go as it pleases.

M r. Lin came to look at my sixties Westinghouse air conditioner that had been lovingly moved from one window to another only to breathe its last on the two days when the heat became suddenly intense. He bent over, peered behind the grill and said, "This machine, no need to fix." I took that to mean "Buy a new one."

There were Japanese air conditioners, and there were the good old American-made Friedrichs. I tried to obtain inside information from Mr. Lin. Wasn't Friedrich the most durable machine? Mr. Lin was noncommittal: "One man make one machine, another man make another machine. One machine work. One machine break. Every machine different. No one can say which machine better. Nobody knows. I cannot tell you. Nobody can tell you."

Mr. Lin sold Carriers and Friedrichs—they were the only brands in his catalogue which contained little black-and-white photographs of some models and their prices. Mr. Lin called a day later saying a client of his was selling a Friedrich he himself had installed that was only a year old and twelve thousand BTUs—more or less what I needed. He said he would bring it, plug it in, and if I liked it, he would install it.

He carted the machine in on a dolly. It was immense and the color of a biscuit. "I made mistake," Mr. Lin said. "It's fourteen thousand BTUs and two years old." The size of it worried me right away but Mr. Lin plugged it in and it seemed to be working fine. I told Mr. Lin I found it very noisy and he said: "After I install, noise stay outside." It was eleven in the morning.

At one in the afternoon the new air conditioner was still on the floor. I caught an exchange between Mr. Lin and his partner Mr. Li that gave me a sense of where the time had been going. They spoke to each other in Chinese but every sentence contained one or two words in English. This is how it sounded to me: "Win wang chaochao wun drill?" for instance, and the reply, "Weh-weh yen-wa driver seat." Mr. Li went downstairs and returned twenty minutes later without the drill. There were more exchanges and more trips by Mr. Li but still no drill. Mr. Lin went down himself. At half past one, the drill having been found, we decided we all needed a break.

When he returned, two hours later, Mr. Lin said he had had to go very far in search of a Chinese restaurant. Meanwhile, a storm had exploded over the city: the sky was dark, there were howling winds and rain and they came in through the open window that no longer had either the old or the new air conditioner in it. The room was chilly.

By six-thirty the new machine was up but there were still two gaps on either side of it. Mr. Lin and Mr. Li would return in the morning, so I cut two strips of cardboard and fitted them over the gaps.

The next day, I turned the machine on to see how it worked. The lowest setting emitted a potent airstream. The cat hid beneath the couch. A pile of paper was lifted up and scattered across the room. I didn't see how I could work in the stream of a typhoon. Mr. Lin confirmed that no lower or quieter setting was possible. I suspected myself of being unreasonable: reasonable people did not quibble over the noise an air conditioner made—one so promisingly named Quietmaster. It must mean, I thought, that other brands were even noisier. I sought once again to extract from Mr. Lin an opinion as to which brand might be quieter. But he went into his philosophical dissertation once again, starting with "Every machine different . . ." and ending with ". . . not possible to know." But then he had a sudden illumination: "Machine very noisy because room very quiet—you writer."

The cat arrived one autumn into my silent house uninhabited except for the anatomy that I see as a continuation of limbs and organisms growing out of the observatory that is my head. I tried the first weeks to think of how I might nicely dispose of him—not kill him, but have him vanish somehow: give him away, for instance. I thought of little else as he tentatively began to proffer his affections, the first timid traces of his forming attachment—an outstretched paw, climbing over my chest and rubbing the side of his head against my jaw and neck. Every sign sank me deeper into responsibility, into disgust at the notion of responsibility.

Hare had said, "Go and see him, then tell me what you think," having spotted him in a pet shop. "Call me from the store," he said. I was in no rush. He had called again: "Have you gone?" Again, I let half an hour elapse.

In the cage the creature was tall on its paws, a puma with turned-down ears like those of a hippopotamus or a bulldog, a round face. It was put in a viewing box, so I might observe and touch him. His very first gesture was to put his paw on my cheek gently. I called Hare. "Buy him," he said immediately, "it will be my gift." He would come in the morning with a credit card. I was grateful to have a night in which to deliberate the decision though I already felt trapped. In the morning I found myself accompanying Hare to the shop, my body walking along willingly, though my mind repeated, *mistake, mistake, mistake.* The reprimand played at the back of my mind for several weeks during which I found it hard to concentrate on my work, found it hard to think of anything at all without the cat being part of it: morning and cat, breakfast and cat, bathe, dress and cat, sit at work table and cat, music and cat, kitchen and cat. Cat everywhere, dependent cat, sleeping leaping caterwauling cat, cat in my destiny, cat on my path, cat in the way. Cat cat cat. Cat needing food. Cat needing litter cleaned. Purring cat. Cute cat—cuteness the most cloying thing of all. Cuteness was meant to have no part in life, one could dismiss it. But here I was faced with the undeniable existence of cuteness. I tried to uncute him, thinking that beneath all that thick grey fur was nothing but flesh, like that of a rabbit ready to be roasted, and bones. Nothing cuddly about the bones of a cat. I called him Plotino (the name, in Italian, of a mystical Greek philosopher, born in Alexandria as I was) for the sound he made when landing on his paws, and the o's were the shape of his head and of his very round eyes.

Nothing noble about having a cat. It was even somewhat pathetic, because it seemed to announce that I had enlisted a small creature to mediate my isolation in the world. A woman living with a cat—pathetic. The voice of cajolement formed at the base of my throat and spoke to him in my place. I watched as though an uninvited guest had entered my frame and spoke in a manner that was not mine. It was not a baby voice but a sort of strangled, high-pitched squeaking voice—a voice of pure libido, of childishness, or of spirit talking to spirit. I had given up scolding having done so once when he jumped on the freshly made bed. I had scolded then with a rusty remembrance of the scold: thundering voice, false authority. It must have sounded awful indeed for he cringed beneath a little table by the bed and for some hours into the evening continued to cringe and avoid me as though he and I had both witnessed an embarrassment. But then my entire behavior towards him was embarrassing. I squeezed him with the desire to squeeze him as though it were his role in the world to be the squeez-able organism at my disposal night and day, in the middle of a sentence for consolation, in the middle of the night for consolation, on coming home. Finally I began to return to my senses and decided I should, out of respect, accord him a certain independence within the confinement of having to live in my house and not being able to go outside. It occurred to me that there should not be much difference between the way one treated a person and an animal. One communicated with them differently, but if one aspired to be independent and grant them independence, there was no difference. I saw him as one who had mysteriously come to share my existence and for whose bodily subsistence I was responsible but that I would not try to influence or bend. I would neither teach, reprimand nor make demands of him. I would learn from him equanimity and the lack of pre-meditation: I would observe cuteness, attempt not to hold it against him. Cute he might be, but tragic, too, destined as he was to a pathetic existence in a Manhattan apartment at my mercy for food, water, shelter. You could say he was a lucky cat for I certainly took his welfare to heart and made sure his feedings were regular, that there were enough little tins of food on hand at all times. He and I—domestic animals.

He took to jumping up on the bed in the early hours of the morning behind my head on the pillow and purring. If I reached out one hand to stroke his head he purred louder. But if my hand was beneath the pillow he took it for a strange disembodied object and grasped it with his paws. Once his claw penetrated deep into my thumb and it bled. What a strange misapprehension that one may undo, reverse, divert the course of things. I disinfected the wound.

Then, in those early hours of the morning, he took to walking over me with a moonwalker's gait, as though surveying land he had purchased: stalking gingerly, one careful paw at a time, like an astronaut on the surface of the moon, and with every stride the undeniable discreet air of the conqueror about him: on my chest, if he could have, he would have planted a flag. He might as well have done so. Sometimes he put his paw on a quarter of a square inch, like a fraction of the liver, that was tender, and the pain would be acute (*cute* comes from the French *cuit,* which means "boiled down," or is short for *acute,* "something suggesting daintiness, fine features, deftness"), but such was the privilege of this morning promenade that I lay still not wishing to disturb the dancing declaration. Other times, he would merely step into the room with a strangled roar, like a mouse mimicking a lion, to alert me to his presence.

He signalled his satisfaction with circumstances by lying on his stomach with his paws stretched out behind him, as though he were on a beach. And just when I was becoming accustomed to the cat and its cuteness, a large gory crucified Christ came into the house. It was half a person tall; a squat, stocky man, rib cage protruding for the stretching of the arms upwards to the pawish hands nailed to a cross older than the sculpture. The hair sculpted in neat spiralling furrows; the features of the face sharp, the nose thin and bony, the expression placidly aggrieved. From the hairline rivulets of blood ran down the forehead, down the side of the face. Each knee was a spring of blood running down the legs; blood from the side of the chest. The crown of thorns was not a sculpture but was made recently from a double branch spiked with long thorns which made the placing of it on his head almost feel as though one were perpetrating the torture all over again.

Hare hung the cross on a wall to the right of the bed. At first I could not look at it without averting my eyes. I thought that at night the sight of its black mass on the wall would frighten me. I could not look at it without feeling nails being hammered into flesh and bone, the protracted pain of bleeding to death. Christ crucified in my room, the room where I slept, every minute of the day and night. The sight of it, its existence, gripped me as the existence of the cat had done. In every room in the house I saw the Man, his knees bent, his ribs stretched, bleeding, his feet nailed one on top of the other to the base of the cross. The sculpture was cracked over one hip and the opposite shoulder. I considered resting it on the bed for there it might look less crucified, less in pain, but Hare would have none of it. "It is the remnants of your Jewish ancestry that make it hard for you to have a crucifix in the house," he told me: a true Christian is used to seeing a crucifix. I said, "How could a true Christian ever become inured to the sight of a body nailed to a cross and left to a long agony?"

My fear when the cat came was that it would suffer at my hands. I did not consider myself capable of caring for it, and was in no mood to do so. The crucifix needed nothing but a little dusting now and again and perhaps roses placed at its feet once in a while. The first bouquet was of pink roses. Because the object was inanimate, it would submit to my will, which the cat never would. So it was more difficult to honor the cat than the crucifix, easier to have died than to live—at the hands of humans.

I cannot write. I look at the cat. I sit on the canvas sofa and look at the floor, at the streaks left by the hand that had wiped the glass of the window. The neighbor's wooden shutters across the street were open earlier, now they are closed. I see the interminable building next to it that ruins the view and makes up the view. How I always look out and try not to see it, to pretend it isn't there, or to find some saving grace to it, and fail, and fail. The neighbor who washes her clothes and hangs them out on the balcony; floor after floor, the impression that everyone in that building must be looking at me and the inability to see any of them for they live on their section of each floor, quietly, unmovingly, unlookingly. I never see them waking up, opening their windows. They live behind my back, under my nose. I never see their faces except rarely, in fact I only see the lady who hangs her clothes on the balcony, then smokes a cigarette. The building might be uninhabited if it weren't for her. Even on a Sunday afternoon in Manhattan, there is no one. There was a Father's Day when an entire family in three generations huddled on one balcony and it said much about those balconies: they are a conversation piece, something to show the visitors, pointing out that bending forward one can see the park before quickly retiring to the interior. Only the balcony with the green plants has the flowery dress hanging on it and some chairs. I dislike seeing the flowery dress, the man's jacket being aired, or being dirtied in the smog perhaps.

I look at the cat. I play music, taking no special pleasure in it. Perhaps it is too familiar. I wonder if there might be a multitude of things elsewhere that would make my blood race, make me feel as though I were plunged deep into the swift currents of the most vigorous of lives. Instead, I feel engulfed by disinterest, by languor, by the inability to do.

I listen to music that once made me think of Italy and now is part of this New York which contains and excludes every part of the world I have ever known. I play music, and doze, and wait dreamlessly. I expect nothing of myself. I don't think there is anything I was called to do. I could continue so aimlessly, benevolent towards others, inactive towards the world. It's a sunny day but the sky is dull grey, bright and blinding dull grey. I do not use the telephone which once was attached to my ear for hours on end. I think of going to the park to walk.

The shirt is outside my pants. I must go to Turin some time soon for an article. I regret having to leave the cat. I don't quite know how to proceed. In general. My hours are filled with a remote sensation of doubt. It is the opposite of what one might call "nagging" doubt. Do I have enough schooling? I wonder. Is there anything I know how to do? Is there anything I should do? Should I merely learn to cook without salt or without fat? But perhaps it is more healthy to eat a bit of everything. To do a bit of everything. To see a bit of everyone. To stay a little bit everywhere. To be a particle. To dedicate oneself, bit by bit, to the trivial, the marginal, the sidelines of one's very existence, all that happens unlooked at, unnoticed, the immense universe of the "unimportant"—all that one was taught to skip over, gloss over, synthesize, in order to leave space and light to the supposedly essential, the quintessential even. Day by day, I watch myself, seeing myself more and more as unimportant and all that I do along with it and yet giving the unimportance the attention, the time, the reverence of affairs of state, of my affairs of state: The experience, by degrees, of the daily ritual of living as composed of a thousand irrelevancies without which nothing would exist.

I'll have won when I can look at the cat, at the world, too, the way the cat looks at me and at the world—*without intention*. I say I cannot write and yet here I am attempting to record my inability, to let the ineptitude have a voice, let the having nothing to say have nothing to say for itself. Make no excuse for it. The cat is behind me on an armchair that I covered with grey cotton the other day in an attempt to improve the appearance of this room. I sit on a black swiveling chair on casters that I have covered with a piece of crumpled white muslin. It was done much better before I had removed the muslin and hung it from the shade in an attempt to soften the office window appearance of this room. Since it did nothing much for the shades except add messiness to the bleakness, back the cloth went onto the black office swiveling chair on casters, but because it was the second time I did it, there was no spontaneity and the cloth seemed to have been draped on the chair by a teenager eager to personalize a room at any cost with any little piece of rubbish.

I will go to the park, walk around the pond several times,

observe others to see if they might still be having a relevant life, go to the grocery, attempt to be interested in acquiring one or another thing I might cook this evening. "Was there a bomb somewhere?" a man sitting on a sidewalk asks me, glancing at the front page of an ancient newspaper.

I, the djinn, reign over the empty spaces once occupied by her "plans" and "desires." Everything is proceeding according to plan. I find in a manual: "The practitioner next loses his sense of separateness, of the boundaries usually established by the physical body, and the distinction between self and others. Once he has surpassed this distinction he is able to perceive whole hosts of divine beings."

Saying yes in the course of fifteen minutes three times in one morning has gotten her into having lunch with three different people in three different places, albeit near each other and at slightly different hours. So this is what she does: selflessly eats three meals she has no hunger for, attempting to give her guests the freshness he or she deserves. Hare is usually the last invitation and the one she will always accept no matter how many previous commitments there may be for an encounter with Hare is to her a promise of contentment. She has several friends like herself who live by themselves and do not make lunch dates in advance for they do not have that kind of social existence. But when midday comes around they neither like to eat by themselves nor to skip a meal so they call frantically to the few like themselves trying to secure their presence. She receives many such calls because she rarely turns them down and so she is often called first. They do not know of course that she will have three lunches, and there are days naturally when no one calls and lunch, tea, dinner must be had alone.

On that particular three-lunch day she had woken up thinking she needed to take a long journey. She had dreamt of a house by the sea. It was not very large but it over-looked the sea on two sides. She remembered thinking, "Why did I ever leave that place? What made me move away? Did I not realize that that was my sanity?" And now she was reduced to constructing a splendid view out of all the friends she admired, a glimpse of their face somehow comparable to that of the side of a mountain, a pensive brow to a sky, their talk and moods a display of weather, their bodies a landscape. People on that island became to her places and views. So it was that what might have seemed unreasonable—her insatiable appetite for the company of friends—was justified in one after all human. The problem was how to eat so much without bursting. Or how to eat a first course in one place and a second in the second. Then, too, she could not rid herself of a slight guilt towards each of her companions—that she had not dedicated an entire lunch to them to the exclusion of all other solicitations no matter how irresistible they might have been.

The sun has come out and we are about to embark on our dangerous adventure—getting through three engagements without mishap and without being too late for any. On the success of it depends her conquest of a new calm: if she is able to vanquish this dragon in the form of a plot devised by and for her very own insatiability, if she can go through with it feeling no guilt, even less guilt than usual, letting it all up to chance, she will have come that much closer to my creed, "No struggle, no speed, no hope, no fear."

THREE

PRISONER OF A DREAM

In the dream, his house is a castle enveloped in darkness. He may be in it somewhere, but I never know in which room. I make my way in the dark careful not to wake Maro who may be asleep in the room with Hare beneath a painted green field. Sometimes she is not there at all, but I have no way of knowing. I creep down long corridors, into unlit rooms, my arms outstretched to feel for the form of a bed. When I find it, I lie down hoping no one will surprise me in it. I lie awake listening to noises in the house. I hear steps. At times I am certain that they are his steps and long to call out, but that I must not do. Once or twice Maro awakes, comes into my room. I hear her breathing. I am certain she will walk over to my bed but before she has a chance to, I tiptoe out of the room, down the stairs, out of the house, across the garden, into the fields, into the night, so she will not find me.

I love to watch him dress: turquoise shirt and green tie, red wool scarf, black Afghan hat. His universe pays a visit to mine—tie, shirt, trousers, shoes, crumpled socks on the floor. He leaves them all outside our bed which is covered by a frail Portuguese embroidery and a black Mexican blanket, rasping as the hair of goats.

The March Hare, place of the present. Pink orchids, pink

roses, red carnations. The Princess, his mother, is here, all eighty-nine years, belittling him with every other breath, thinking to solve the obvious: He has too much to do in too many places, she decrees; eliminate one—Mexico, for instance, all bandits and dust anyway.

She cannot know I found him perfect as recently as seven hours ago. I bury my eyes and nose in the flesh of his chest and it is the way to go inside my head, with the sound of a beating pulse and the colors in the eyes of blood running through his skin and mine jammed together, unbreathing, constricted. I could stay, or go up into where a quivering line forms then I never wait too long to let it go and fall into the end. Singing little sleep, feeling no part, arm, head, leg, neck, privileged over another, democracy and order restored among the blood cells, one brain ticking modestly at the service of all. But he is not happy, doesn't think he is.

At dinner at his house, the first time we met, my eyes fell on his hand. A circle of wooden chairs around a small table at the center of an oblong room, stained-glass windows, a painting of bubbling white and blue drop-shaped molecules magnified a million times and another of a man and a woman's faces side by side, rabbit-eared. Also, a globe-shaped painted face with baby's breath for hair and a white plaster shadow of a gentleman with a bomber hat. Walk me home. He said, "Another time," took my number, and I waited two years. There was a son, I found out, a woman, and a baby. But he was here alone. Why?

"This ain't about heaven, it's about me!" yelled a man on a bicycle in Central Park. The Princess's frail tanned hand, mother-of-pearl lacquered and clipped nails, in the crook of my elbow; the brown flannel Givenchy dress Hare disapproved of because it had slits up the sides and her black slip showed through. We walked along. I was pleased for this fragment of family.

I met her son, I finally told her, and two years later he called, on his birthday. Then he returned to Mexico to marry the mother of his two children. Every summer I stayed at the castle for ten days, when Maro preceded Hare to Mexico, and every year I noticed that there weren't any new pots in the kitchen, a picture on the wall that wasn't his or a new piece of furniture. The only signs of her were a flowery dressing gown on the door of the closet, creams in the bathroom and for some time the empty box of a diaphragm, and once by his bed a bracelet. The presence of that bracelet in his bedroom had poisoned my mind because out of gallantry to her he had refrained from telling me that he was being faithful. Jealousy does not need fact to feed on since it can gorge on conjecture.

The Princess and I clambered high up into the gazebo in the park and there observed the tops of trees. She dwelt on her morning tremor. "It's better in the afternoon," she said. She took an aspirin and that helped. Was there any relation between that and the cancer in her? That question obsessed her. "Will you come with me to look for lipstick one day?" she asked. "The one I have on is Dior, it was the best I could find." We went in search of her favorite, Coral Melon by Estée Lauder, which was an acid pink-orange color.

I liked the Princess immediately, her uncluttered ways, her

determination to rid conversation of tedium, precisely as if she were writing.

But in the seven months that she was here to receive radiation treatment, there was a strain between us at times when I took her to the hospital because she did not always feel well.

A woman in her eighties endowed with a brilliant intellect she put at the service of conversation and memory, the Princess was born in Tuscany of an aristocratic family, moved to Rome as a young girl and lived there most of her life aside from a spell in England and summers at the seaside resort of Forte dei Marmi. She married a writer and had three children. She did not have what is known as a career, aside from the self-determined one of listening to artists and writers, to their stories and jokes, and committing the best of what she had witnessed to memory. She was a fixative of spirits.

The first time we met was in Rome some fifteen years ago. The Princess received me in her apartment on the Via Gregoriana which over the years had been progressively reduced by her landlords who lived in the same building. They took from her one large room, then another, till she had two bedrooms, a small parlor by the entrance and a tiny room off the kitchen with long communicating corridors in between whose windows gave onto a central courtyard. One heard the gurgling of a fountain from below bringing fresh spring water.

We sat in the little parlor, side by side on a settee, sipping vermouth in a glass the size of a thimble. When she poured, it was clear the Princess could not see well. But her movements were as precise as her sentences, her mind as lucid as her memory. We drained one glass, then two more. The Princess propped a glass ashtray between us and we smoked one cigarette after another. Two hours passed in which we gave each other a tour of the funnier stories at our disposal. The Princess wore a thick blue jersey shirt-waist dress with a black patent leather belt slung low on the hips which I came to recognize as her style and had no doubt begun in the sixties. Her hair, cut to the lobes and combed back, was a blond caramel color. She wore foundation to hide some of the brown spots on her face for she had spent much time in the sun. Her wardrobe consisted of Courrèges, Givenchy, Saint Laurent, her mental furnishings of Shakespeare, Leopardi, Chekhov, Pound. The latter had been a friend of her husband's.

After two hours, we parted and on the train to Florence, later that evening, I sat reviewing the encounter and feeling as though I had fallen in love.

For many years, I was just this—a person to whom the Princess told stories and I, too, tried my fresh ones on her knowing I had found my ideal audience. Returning from journeys to Jordan, Vietnam, or Egypt, I would stop in Rome and tell the Princess every new anecdote, making sure I made them comical enough for her—such as that of the man on a plane who had confided to me, "Kabbalah is *verry vallable* because it is almost infallible!" There was no obligation between us: we were free to carry on our friendship in whatever fashion suited us and so we conducted it far from the routines of family. We had dinner at the Chinese restaurant down the street, took long walks to the Villa Borghese and had ice cream at the bar of the Casina Valadier. Sometimes I would spend a night at the Princess's house before proceeding on my travels and in the morning she would bring me breakfast on a tray, carefully laid out with a blue-and-white china cup and plate.

It was only much later, when the Princess fell ill, that I became her cook, companion, daughter. A daughter who could lull her into thinking she could be a good mother because none of the constraints and duties were there to spoil the fun, to hold up the mirror to the Princess's inability to take an interest in poor dependent creatures, such as the actual members of a family. The Princess and I were characters in a play who would be allowed to go home by themselves at the end of the evening, rest, take a bath and the next day return to their parts refreshed, ready to give the best of themselves, give what was demanded, demanding nothing in return, like actors who don't have to be anyone in between roles. To be the accepted, recognized member of a family is to be obliged to be "oneself," complying with others' memories and one's own habits, day after day. As "mother," "father," "son," "daughter," one was a service rather than a moveable feast of organisms, the inside of a point of view, a point from which to view the world, and see what the day, and each moment in it, would bring.

She said, "Frivolity is everything in life. And the place where one feels best is at the hairdresser, and at the bank: there is a sense of concrete things there."

A man at the entrance to the park bared his belly to the sun: a large flaccid belly that he rested on the bench by him as he read the paper, a belly in different colors of tan dirt and peel and a nest of hair washed perhaps never, matted blond, held back, then a cluster of knots and snags. The Princess had been here nearly a month and hadn't been to the hairdresser since the day before she left and her hair still looked neat—blond and ash, straight, just one lock shorter near the face. She had it cut by Tiziano at De Luca, in Rome. The first time she had gone there she had been eight with long hair that needed trimming. It was considered racy, then, to go to the hairdresser, she told me, so most women had their hair done at home. When she was in high school, the *garçonne* hairstyle was coming into vogue from Paris and she very much wanted to cut her hair but at school they informed her that if she did so the headmaster, an Austrian, wouldn't stand for it. She would risk expulsion. So she waited and cut her hair as soon as she was out of school, to go with her first Chanel suit. "De Luca is like home to me," she said, "more stable than home." It was a place she went to for eighty years. She was born in 1907.

She asked once: "Where were you in 1944?" As if we were the same age.

Her black suede shoes with single noodlelike laces and low square heels were somewhat stained but looked as though they had been carefully brushed. The Princess's universe was marked by this neglect of material things that were once "good" things: good furniture, good clothes, good houses left to fend for themselves as though maintenance were one of their functions.

We went to sit by the pond and observed the movements of a white remote-controlled power boat, a white just-coiffed poodle prancing by with a puff for a tail. A saxophonist played "The Very Thought of You" at a dirgelike tempo. Leaves detached from branches by a breeze were beginning to float off into the air and down to the ground but the trees were still mostly green. Blue sky and mild air. "This is a strange city," the Princess said after a bit. "One doesn't know whether it is today, tomorrow, a hundred years from now, or a hundred years ago—it is quite unreal."

She had asked for a painting by Morandi, instead of a ring, as an engagement gift from her husband. Years later they had lent it to a gallery for an exhibition and the gallery had inadvertently sold it. The painter had offered them another but they never went to retrieve it in Grizzana Morandi, the little town near Bologna where the painter lived, and so the gift was lost.

The family fortune at any rate consisted of the stories they told—anecdotes made into stories by one or another member, faithfully remembered and rendered by the others. The exact wording, timing, effects were repeated. The mother, her daughter, the eldest son all told them, and to be initiated into their family was to be told those stories.

A writer they often visited was known for offering one nothing to eat or drink except if one stayed over two hours; then he would say, "Would you like a glass of water?" or, "Would you like a sardine? It comes in a tin, very simple, really." No one ever accepted these offers and the only man who dared stay until dinner time caught the writer's wife shaking her head violently from the kitchen at her husband to indicate that even the sardines were out of the question.

Whenever it rained, they quoted an officer at the front during the First World War who, when it rained, would say forlornly, "It's raining, and old Doddoli isn't even here." Among their close friends was a famous professor who could not be named as the mere naming of him could cause the electrical wiring to short-circuit, earthquakes, floods, and other cataclysms no one dared think of.

The daughter imitated a fellow actor-in-training who recited a scene from *Julius Caesar*. He would stand aghast like one whose foot had been trod on by a donkey and mutter in a thick Romanesque accent, "Oy, it's Caesar's corpse!" Then she would reenact the scene of a stranger she had encountered on the street one evening who had muttered lustily to her, "I'd like to sink my teeth into you."

I see the blurred white wave of the sheet, his ear, an inch of neck, pull my pillow closer to his, and put my arm around his chest: why was I afraid of this? I upheld the virtues of inconstancy, unmonotony, unduty, and having done so, was afraid to try the half-married life—he is still at the Gloomy Castle, I am here, at the new treehouse, but Maro is gone.

He turned around and drew my head to him so that the right side of my face was pressed against his chest and I breathed out of my left nostril. I fell asleep again, one of my arms beneath me, the hand bent backwards, the fingers gathered in a beak, and I let it go numb—so what. The phone rang, I didn't answer.

Sitting at the table in Hare's dining room, the Princess looked at the painting of two feet nailed down, perhaps to a cross like Christ's, and said, "I don't like that painting, never have." Then we inspected a staff on the other table which was cluttered with stacks of books and surrounded by a conference of Hare's jackets slung on the backs of chairs. The backs of the chairs were narrower than Hare's shoulders so the creases made the jackets seem to be shrugging. The staff was a Masai staff Hare received from his son Moon who had gone to Africa and seen "one tiger, and one hippopotamus," the Princess said, expressing her disapproval of such displacements. It was a disapproval she threw at all the lands untouched by the age of enlightenment: Africa, India, Australia, certainly Latin America, and, of the European countries, Spain, which she said was responsible for bringing the Mafia to Naples. England she admired though she recalled the newspaper headline that said, "The Continent Isolated," when on account of the fog all navigation was suspended between England and "the continent," Europe. I think she believed the rest of the world to be isolated with respect to Italy.

Pushkin, the landlord, was at the door to measure the space for the fridge. Meanwhile it made a low purring sound. Pushkin seemed impatient when I asked, since he was getting me a smaller fridge, could he not also try for a quieter one. People like Pushkin think it's fastidious to dwell on such details. But noise is not a detail. For seven years I tried to persuade the whistling morning doorman of the hotel across the street not to whistle. Once I approached him about it, and as I did so, he backed away as though I were brandishing a weapon.

An albino grasshopper fell into the abyss between a raised window and a lowered one above the air-conditioning unit, onto a wad of white tissues blackened by soot put there to muffle the draft. Hare brought me white and indigo irises—sixteen stalks. The movement of my hand reflected in the tin cover on the teapot startled me as though I had caught sight of another presence in the room, standing behind me looking on.

Driving rain torrented out of the gutter around the roof and came down in an avalanche in front of the door to the terrace, swamping and crushing the geranium. I dared not go out to save the plant or my poor roses that were on the point of blooming. The sky was dark and felt foreign. The yellow blooms drooped sadly. I would cut them off when the deluge stopped.

I looked at the photograph of Hare by my bed. I saw a new face whenever I looked, and the new face I had grown overnight tending the wounds of the previous day, caressing the new skin that had grown over them, greeted his. The word "love" fails at the very start of anything that might prove to be that. All around it is a field of reserve, antagonism, suspicion—a swamp of yearning to be well, have company, audience, peace. The other is on an abandoned horizon painted by desire and unlike a single pore of the person one has yet to discover, every day a new millimeter.

I watched the wind and thought I would stay home. Patience is almost everything.

The doctor explained the Princess's medical predicament. The cancer was "eating" its way through her. There were only about five millimeters between the bladder and the womb, which, he said, if only I could see it in an anatomical drawing, was a masterpiece. A certain Doctor Gilliatt, gynecologist to Her Majesty the Queen of England, probably at the end of the thirties, to whom the Princess had been referred by the Italian ambassador, had told her that she was the most admirably constructed woman he had ever seen. She added, "He meant from a gynecological point of view," to temper the boast.

The problem was to sink the Princess's ship of cancer without sinking the canal it was moored in. The doctors met to decide on her medical treatment, if any, and she seemed not to find it ominous that they might conclude it was best to do nothing at all. She didn't read the medical finality of that, even thought it a reassuring possibility. One doctor said, "In America, doctors believe if you're over seventy-five, you're not worth treating." But the picture of cells withdrawn from within the Princess travelled from specialist to specialist. Again she asked what the tremor might be. One doctor thought it might be anxiety. "That's right," she nodded, "anxiety—or cervical arthritis. Perhaps there's something I could take."

The hemorrhage was due to the cancer having infiltrated

a little vein. If the cancer were to reach an artery, the bleeding would be extreme and could lead to death. If nothing were done, she would die in one to four years. If she were given "highly targeted" radiation that penetrated the skin, reached the affected area and burned it, she could live a few more years. There was, though, one chance in a thousand that the radiation might cause a tear impossible to repair for at least a year because the surrounding tissue would have to expel all the radiation before any surgery could be attempted and there was enough healthy tissue to effect the healing. If she were to have either a spontaneous tear in the wall of the vagina due to the cancer, or one brought on by the radiation, urine would flow out, and that would be an untenable way to live for someone like the Princess. I explained to her only that the loss of blood might have brought on the feeling of dizziness she had been experiencing.

She came to lunch. We had penne with zucchini, steamed endives, and a mille-feuille apple tart she loved. We discussed Polynesia. One had to fly to Bora-Bora first and that was only thirty-nine square kilometers. From there one took a motorboat ride across a lagoon to Vahine. There was nothing but a set of small bungalows that comprised the hotel, and the island seemed to have no inhabitants except for the hotel's four employees and whatever guests might be on hand. Hare's best friend, Ruy, who had been there years before, said Bora-Bora was a favorite of couples on their honeymoon and that it was quite boring. As for the Polynesians, he considered them legumes: big and empty. The

Princess was indignant at this stricture: "One cannot expect aborigines to be amusing," she said sternly. "Curious, perhaps. At any rate, one would have to speak their language to find out what is in their head." As for the trip, she did not advise it: "All tropical places resemble each other, what need is there to travel so far?"

As I cooked, the Princess had her customary shot of scotch, neat, sitting on the couch, listening to a Haydn cello concerto, in her navy blue Courrèges suit with frog ties. Her hair was out of kilter, but she was as sharp as ever. We had walked over, and when I realized she was having trouble keeping up with me, I slowed down. Every now and then we stopped to look at shop windows so she might catch her breath. We looked at black lace underwear on mannequins, and she commented, "Not bad, but I never did like lace; I always try to find simple underwear without frills. I get them at Upim." Upim was a popular department store in Rome. She looked at the minimalist acid-green windows of a Prada boutique and asked, "Is that a discount store?"

Time and the Princess: she made it collapse like a house of cards. I had picked her up at one-thirty, and when I next looked at my watch it was five o'clock. Conversation was her occupation, and it was therefore her skill to find at every turn something to talk about, to weave a tapestry of words over an entire afternoon, hour after hour, finding subjects to entertain herself and others with. The hours passed on a bubbling stream of talk and the landscape on its banks did not hold surprises or threats. Little by little the sensation began to take hold that nothing was so essential that it actually needed to be done. "She would have liked us to be ornaments," Hare once said.

Heavy rain on the leaves and the sound of Indian flutes. Hare took the Princess to the doctor, one who had tended to her years ago, and he, too, withdrew a sample of tissue. The Princess bled profusely. In a week they would "know." So the decision as to what her treatment would be was once again postponed, as was her return to Italy. The doctor told her to douche but gave her no prescription. I promised Hare I would buy the "contraption." The box contained a little diagram of a thin woman lying naked in a bathtub (titled "How to take effective douches"). Her hand, which was between her thighs, was drawn in a dotted line (as one was not meant to be able to see it, since she was portrayed in profile) and held a long nozzle inside her. "Hold the labia closely around the nozzle for one minute," the instructions read, "to induce a slight ballooning of the vagina." The Princess groaned, "What a complication!" The outlined woman's head reclined on the pillow gracefully and was slightly tilted towards the eye of the draughtsman. She was by herself, but furtive, as though she knew someone might be watching from a hidden vantage point—precisely the way one feels performing such rituals. The Princess bemoaned the lack of bidets in America, then she quoted the first sentence of one of Alberto Moravia's short stories, " 'I used to be a plumber,' " and giggled.

We went to the park and walked towards the Metropolitan Museum. An English professor she and her husband had known declared one day that he, his wife, and their daughter had decided to become nudists. "I wonder what made them do it," she said. "From one day to the next they started ambling about the house without any clothes on. Why? To return to their origins, to feel free of sin, like Adam and Eve perhaps?"

Back on our street, we saw a man get into an old pea-green Mercedes we had often observed parked by the curb. "I like cars," she said. "They are such inventions, but you need a driver just to take care of them." In London, she and her husband had had a Jaguar, and when they sold it, they interviewed prospective buyers to make sure whoever bought it would take proper care of it. In Rome, they had a Lancia Augusta, and during the war a drunk German officer once stopped her and asked her to get out, saying that he was requisitioning it. She was with her three children, and while another officer went to fetch some documents, she calculated that he would not be back for a number of seconds. The Princess's driver pushed the drunk officer over the side of the road and they drove off.

The verdict came: the Princess was to have three weeks of radiation—every day, five days a week, in the morning at eleven. It would be done at New York Hospital. She was very disappointed that all three doctors had reached the same conclusion, having hoped that no treatment would be necessary. The external radiation was intended to erect a barrier around the area where the cancer had developed. It was not targeted at the growth itself.

We had chicken cutlets and asparagus, spinach, cauliflower, then watched television and learned that O. J. Simpson had been acquitted of the murder of his wife and her friend. Hare remembered two brothers and a sister who liked getting tied to a bed and tickled. Their father complained, "They take their little sister and shove her into the wall."

I hurtled out the door to get a thin apple tart, mushrooms for a risotto, yellow and red peppers and basil. The dishwasher had a few clean plates and glasses in it I had to take out. I dove under the sink looking for a small frying pan, and the big one fell, followed by a saucepan, then two lids, clatter, clatter. . . . I held on to my T-shirt and with my mouth shut, yelled without yelling, just compressed hot air pushed into the stomach. I took one of the steel lids and threw it onto the pile of pots, took it out and threw it again, with relish. I wondered if I had Tourette's syndrome. It is supposed to be augmented by stress. A cook's stress. I was trying to make a nice lunch for Hare and the Princess but I had only forty minutes to do so. I didn't say, "No, it's too late." I said, "Fine. Wonderful."

They arrived with a cake brought to them by a guest a few days before. The Princess came to the kitchen and admired the new fridge. She said, "It makes the whole kitchen look bigger. Your landlord Pushkin really put himself out." Then she added absentmindedly, "I wonder if the doctors know just what those radiations are like. Maybe we could ask?" I stirred the rice as she sat on the square white trash can, her legs crossed, an ashtray propped on one knee, a chalice of straight scotch in one hand.

"Pound would have a siesta after lunch, in the brief time he was in Rome," she said, "and he would return from it reading a canto. But then he went to his wife's castle in Trentino, and there he became very thin—he weighed only forty kilos, he'd eat nothing but a leaf of salad, and he hardly spoke anymore. Finally Olga Rudge came to get him, and he went with her to Venice." Pound had exchanged over a hundred letters with the Princess's husband, who had later given them to an assistant to keep; the man had burned them all at the time of Pound's confinement in Pisa, thinking they might be incriminating to the professor. Only a few, of which the poet had kept a copy, survived and were at Yale.

Pound liked to entertain the Princess on the subject of his economic theory: he called it "melting currency," *moneta fondente*—a currency that devalued itself automatically so that in the end it would be worth nothing at all: that would encourage spending and discourage accumulation. It was a countercapitalist approach. The Princess told him it was like an Italian game of cards called the Moor, in which the jack of spades is the one card one must not be caught holding when the game is over or it counts for many points that are added up with the player's final hand.

She liked the peppers very much, called them a masterpiece. I washed the saucepans, put the dishes in the dishwasher, wiped the counter, made coffee, put little dried apricots in a dish, the dish and the cups on a round aluminium tray with a square white linen napkin on it.

We had coffee. Hare retreated into a nervous solitude sitting at the head of the table by himself, by the open window to the terrace where several pale yellow roses had bloomed that very morning. He rushed us: we had to go and see a show of new paintings. He wanted to include the Princess, and yet once he had done so, he sometimes found her presence suffocating. In the street, he walked ahead, making us feel very slow indeed, every now and then turning to see if we were following him. I tried to distract him by talking to him, but he walked ahead unseeingly.

The Princess entered the elevator and admired, half-mockingly, its solid brass interior. In the gallery, she went to sit on a low bench. She was wearing her Saint Laurent cobalt-blue wool blouse, a blue skirt, and her usual low-slung black patent leather belt. When she had recovered her breath, she went to peer at every painting in the face, only there were no faces: they were portraits of egg-heads in costume—pleated and starched white collars, brocade capelets, billowing skies, and no faces. The Princess sniffed indignantly, "Are they apocalyptic or silly? I hope they're just silly." A strange combination: she understood the paintings and despised them at the same time.

"Have we been sufficiently *épaté*? Can we go now?" she inquired sardonically.

The Princess was made to lie under an octagonal sky-colored panel with a brilliant light at the center of it and geometric drawings, like a constellation, all around. The X-ray unit took images of her abdomen, then many little injections she barely felt were adminstered to the lower part of her belly, hips, and sides. She was to have a CAT scan, then the schedule of radiations would be planned.

"I was in science fiction from twelve to two," she said when she emerged from the panelled room. The technician grumbled that it would only have taken five minutes if she had kept still. The Princess protested, "There are times when one is agitated, but I wasn't, I was perfectly still." She described the procedure: "Huge contraptions draw near the face, then travel up and down one's body. I asked the technician what he saw and he said everything was fine." It sounded like a battle with her body as the battleground on which little red flags were being planted to indicate the places that would come under attack. "I do have the little red flags," the Princess said excitedly. "The other day they made drawings in dark ink on my hips which I have to be careful not to wash off."

There were black flecks on the pink enamel of the sink on the days that Hare woke up at the treehouse and I saw them when I bent low over the sink to rinse my face. I leant forward, expecting nothing but to be absorbed in the act of splashing water on my skin, and a wave of intensity flooded me at the sight of those discarded traces of him that looked like iron dust.

"Yes, he's very good, the mongrel," the Princess conceded reluctantly at the third painting by Mondrian she scrutinized at the Museum of Modern Art. We walked from blue-white to yellow-white to grey-white, and red and blue squares and rectangles dancing about the edge of a picture along straight black dividing lines. "This may not be a religious subject," she said in front of a tree painted like lace over a leaden sky, "but it is equally sublime—not like that painter of egg-faced portraits we saw the other day, trying to be ironic." "Art must edify," she repeated her conviction. "And did you know," she said in front of a black-and-white portrait of the long-faced, triangular-nosed Mondrian at the exit, "he always went dancing, even when he was quite ill? He was an admirer of jazz."

One branch of the rose on the terrace had a pale delirious bloom on it that bent down to the ground, curtsying low— it might have been me. Hare left for Mexico and called from the airport. The radiations were postponed to after his return. Two of the doctors seemed in no hurry to administer them and so the Princess's sojourn was prolonged. I wished that the sweetness of that autumn might have been prolonged, too. The Princess gave us depth, her illness behind the scenes, her age incurring respect, not so much for her as for the moments we could spend with her, for the gaiety that was her way of dispelling the moments of terror she preferred to bear alone.

Hare's best friend Ruy knew how to tell stories to amuse the Princess. Just his blue-eyed, strong-chested presence seemed to have a beneficial effect on her, gave her a reason to dress a little more than usual, apply a little more lipstick, turn the effects of her own anecdotes up a notch.

The first story he told: There was a self-taught young scholar, known for his library of rare books, some of which he had inherited from his grandfather, and some which he was thought to have stolen from public libraries, including the Bibliothèque Nationale. But then he gave up stealing books in favor of stealing saints' relics. He would go to a monastery, an abbey, or a church and emerge with a few precious bone fragments concealed in the lining of his jacket. For his wedding, he wore a doge's habit, a long brown gown, and golden shoes. Just before the ceremony was to begin, he summoned Ruy to him. It was to offer him some hosts that he had stolen so they might take their own communion, but Ruy refused, saying he wasn't even bap-tized. Some time later, the scholar rented a studio near Neuilly that he said was a laboratory. He was building an instrument there, a sort of lute made of stone and measur-ing three meters by one. Was it a sculpture? Ruy asked. The scholar said no, gruffly. Was it an instrument he could play? And the scholar repeated no, even more gruffly. Whatever it was, he kept it to himself, and if one was unable to guess, one was not entitled to know.

The second story: There was a wealthy man with philanthropic tendencies. Hare thought Ruy should meet him to discuss a series of books he was interested in publishing at the time. They both went to dinner at the man's house one night. He had a wealthy Austrian wife with icy eyes. The immense apartment—the walls, piano, rugs, furniture—were all brown. After dinner, Hare stood up, saying he had an urgent engagement. Ruy also stood up but Hare stayed him with one hand, saying, "No need for you to go yet," to the horror of Ruy who was then obliged to remain alone. His host led him through a dark corridor into the study. He showed him two shrouded stacks of paper: one was the story of his life, he said, from the age of five to the age of fifteen, the other was from the age of fifteen to the age of twenty-five. As they were making their way back to the living room, a strange roar was heard, as of a lion or some other wild beast. "Quiet, Bull!" the man hissed. Ruy was perplexed. "Bull, did you say? You keep a bull here?" The man led him to an enormous cage, and pacing in it was an enormous black dog by the name of Bull.

The third story: The Greek Orthodox priest listened to his shortwave radio. When he was in Houston, he stayed home and watched television all day long. On either side of him were little piles of books by Saint John of the Cross and others. He watched and read simultaneously. He wore shoes called Mephisto. Once one of his disciples had fallen in love with a young woman and the priest told him: "It's a gift from God, accept it, but don't become attached to it." The man said, "How can you talk to me? Have you ever touched a woman?" The priest answered cryptically, "I have known women."

He had been known to stop one woman who was staying in the same house as he, a guest of the same benefactress, and ask her a string of questions about her private life. The woman at first cordially answered his questions but soon found his curiosity morbid.

A plate rattled against a pot in the dishwasher. It had been raining all day. The petals of one rose had dropped to the ground in a pale tender mound. One side of the tree was bare, leaving the dry seedpods exposed, and the leaves that would fall in the next few days had yellowed.

Calm down, I told myself, everything is as it should be.

The Princess called and said, "I am prisoner of a dream." She had once heard a prisoner singing the song, which was a popular ballad at the time, as she walked past the Roman prison of Regina Coeli. A melancholy note told me she meant it a little bit though she laughed. "It's so damp, you should not disturb yourself to come all the way here, though perhaps later . . ." I did not know whether pride made her call me before I could call her as though to say she did not need me. But we were on the telephone and our voices began to talk to each other unthinkingly. She remembered a friend who used to have to jump off a running train to go and visit the woman he loved; he did it at a particular place each time when the train slowed down. Had he stayed on, the train would have taken him far beyond the little town that was his destination. The man and his lover ordered cases of champagne which they drank when they were together.

He also smoked a great deal. He died at the age of fifty-two because he was a passionate man, the Princess said.

Those few days before her treatments began felt like the last of a holiday. Autumn continued, mild, almost tropical. Pink roses had bloomed again on the terrace, even more lovely against the fallen yellow leaves, the baring branches, the wet blackish wood of the deck, the forlorn sky.

I slept in Hare's bed for the first time since Maro had gone to Mexico and woke up looking fondly on the collapsing curtains that had been collapsing for years. I saw them and was at home. The picture of the woman with a red leaf at her groin; that of two children copulating, their eyes round, black, and blank—intensely erotic and still. Home.

Cereal. A slice of pumpkin cheesecake left over from the night before. On the way back to the treehouse, I resisted the begging of a young beggar woman who in the summer wore a halter dress cut out of a black plastic garbage bag, but now, in a black leather blouson and jeans, walked in a circle, leaning towards an imaginary center, to look mad or because she was, then followed me with determination for more than two blocks making perfect sense: "Have you ever been hungry? I just want to get something to eat. One day, you, too, could be hungry."

On the way to the Stich Radiation Center with the Princess, I ran into the very doctor who some years before had given me the test diagnosing trisomy of chromosome 21, mongolism, in the fetus I was carrying and had assisted me in delivering it stillborn in the course of a long July night in a room upstairs, overlooking the river, in the Women's Lying-In Hospital. He saw me, looked away, but I knew somehow that he had recognized me. I said, "Hello, Doctor," and used his name. He gave me the briefest of smiles, as warm as I think he knew how to be, and walked on. I explained to the Princess who he was. She said, "I was so sorry when Hare told me. But maybe there is still time." I said, "Well, we can't all have children. And it would have been complicated for Hare at the time." She was resolute: "That shouldn't have had any bearing on the matter."

A doctor friend of hers used to say that knowing all that could happen at conception, all the genes that might interfere, it was a miracle children were ever born normal.

The Princess went to change into a hospital gown, with blue and yellow squiggles on it and open at the back. She said, "I think there are some armchairs outside where one can wait." I understood she wanted me to wait in the reception area so I wouldn't see her undressed.

When I picked her up, she was coughing and her eyes were clouded. She'd had a falling out with Hare that morning and to make matters worse had lost one of her magnifying lenses. She used two to read—at the time, the *Critique of Pure Reason* by Kant—a flat one, and an even stronger spherical one. I promised to inquire about a certain magnifying machine for reading. Hare was all for buying it immediately. He did not say anything to the Princess but made small gestures of reconciliation: "There is not much need to say anything," he said. "She understands right away."

Pushkin, the landlord, insisted on putting mousetraps beneath my radiators. They were very small traps called Victor, hence the red *V* on the unvarnished wooden base. Since the day he had placed them, snapping one by mistake onto his own fingers, I checked them every morning to make sure a mouse hadn't been caught and was decomposing. Pushkin had said, "You'll know if one has been caught by the smell." I was always happy to find the traps empty. But one morning there was a mouse in a trap beneath a radiator, where I had seen it vanish some days before, after it had made a leisurely visit to the center of the room to feast on crumbs from dinner the night before. The Princess, who was not obsessed with hygiene but had enough scientific knowledge to appreciate cleanliness and once argued at the Gloomy Castle that if the cat's dish was being washed in the dishwasher the temperature of the water would not be hot enough to disinfect it, asked precise questions as to the when and how of that visit. Had it been repeated? *How long ago* did you say it was? etc. I found the creature, its neck snapped by the lever of the trap and at that very point the body had been flattened to the thickness of a sheet of paper as though life and soul had been pushed out of it in that one massive blow. Its fur was grey and longer than I expected—I forced myself to look because though I had not set the traps, had even tried to resist them, in the end I had allowed them, so I should see what I had done and dispose of it, too. He had a little white fleck on his forehead and looked like a sleeping mouse but not a real one, somehow. Death had given him the nature of a cartoon mouse—one that can never be killed no matter the aggression, be it dynamite or a hand grenade. His eyes were closed as though death had simply put him into a deep slumber and a blissful one at that. When with a sheet of paper towel I lifted him with the trap from behind the radiator grill, I felt a terrible cringing of sorriness. After the mouse burial, I spent the better part of the morning thinking about the Princess's eyes: a closed-circuit television existed that enlarged the pages of a book onto a screen so that someone with poor eyesight might read.

Waiting for the Princess at the hospital, I picked up a sheaf of clippings regarding the oncologist in whose charge she was. He had pioneered a treatment called brachytherapy which involved placing radioactive pellets directly into a cancerous tumor so as to combat the tumor while harming as few healthy cells as possible. The therapy was actually suggested in the early 1900s, after Madame Curie's discovery of radium, by Alexander Graham Bell: he recommended that radiation be put at the center of a tumor. The procedure was now called 3-D conformal radiation therapy and combined radiation with computer technology. I told her all this and she said, "And I was just imagining how many healthy cells were being killed by each dose of radiation!"

I continued to read: "Nearly all patients who receive treatment for cancer feel some degree of emotional upset. It's not unusual to feel depressed, afraid, angry, frustrated, alone, or helpless. Radiation therapy may affect the emotions indirectly through fatigue or changes in hormone balance, but the treatment itself," it concluded inexplicably, "is not a direct cause of mental distress." The day Hare lost his temper, the Princess said, "I am unhappy." Normally she would have been combative.

One of the Princess's doctors came by and stood in the

doorway. He had dyed his hair a shade of lilac and the hair closer to the hairline was white. He looked out from above his glasses which contributed to a general look of weariness. One's faith in medicine was not improved by meeting him. He leant over and whispered, "How is it going—any bleeding?" The Princess shook her head, "No, very little." "It should go away with the treatment," he said. She retrieved a small folded sheet from her bag and said, "I have been taking medication for the pressure"—she pronounced it *deh pressure*—"and I have only five pills left." "Depression?" the doctor asked. "I'll give you a prescription for Prozac—it works well for depression." "Oh, very good," the Princess murmured, "and it has the same composition?" She proffered the instruction sheet that came in every box of medicine in Italy, but he hardly looked at it before vanishing down the corridor. She put the folded sheet back into her unclutterd black handbag and I noticed that it contained a candid pair of white cotton panties, I suppose in case of accidents. I was surprised to hear the Princess admit to depression, but then when she said *"pressione,"* in Italian, I realized she had meant blood pressure rather than depression and rushed after the doctor. The Princess said, "I knew I had heard of that Prosec somewhere." Prosecco is a bubbly champagnelike white wine; she thought the entire incident very funny.

I brought her some playing cards with numbers printed very large, and she dismissed them, "I despise cards," though Hare had told me it was once a favorite pastime. And when I mentioned a catalogue I had obtained of items for people with poor eyesight, she said, "I suppose it might be useful to people who can't see." But later at the artist's, when Hare said, "I brought two packs, one of Italian playing cards, and the other"—then hesitated, not wanting to offend the Princess, she finished the sentence triumphantly— "for people who can't see, like me!"

The artist moved his Basquiat paintings into one room— they were all of black masks or stylized skulls. He wore burgundy corduroy baggy pants, a reddish shirt, a dull orange wool vest, and said, "My daughter said it's a disgusting combination of colors—I was so pleased with it."

We had dinner around a white formica table: penne with mushrooms and parsley; *stracotto,* beef stewed in wine, and broccoli rabe sautéed in garlic and oil, the latter made by the artist's father as well as the dessert of sliced apples on a hard crust. Then they played cards: Ruy, Hare, the artist, and his wife, as the Princess and I watched.

The Princess smoked some American Spirit cigarettes she found on the table and tilted her head to the Neapolitan songs of Pino Daniele on the cassette player. "I don't give a damn," he was singing.

At the castle, the Princess and I waited for the elevator to return, admiring the ruby red of the light signalling that it was in movement. We entered the cubicle and pressed "1." There was a wooden stool piled with books, bits of mail, and every day the pile rose higher, just as every day the jackets Hare divested himself of onto the backs of chairs increased. That day there were four—three next to each other, looking like underlings called to task at a meeting by the solitary one at the head of the table. The shrugging gave them a skeptical appearance as though in their conference they discussed problems that could not be solved. On the table in front of them were many books, learned journals—it was not a lighthearted state of affairs. They seemed to be negotiating an impossible war. Supersonic planes were going by and it sounded as though they were cruising a foot above the roof of the house, making a crashing noise till it felt as though the windows would burst.

We sat on the flowery couch, with the tall black nose on the right, a totem, and a sculpture that looked like an eruption of lead pouring out of the center of the earth; a row of wooden masks on the piano, one with a long beak, another with eyes and mouth slanted downwards in utter sorrow; a painting of blue doodles on a white background and next to it, on a very long wall, a kind of *Guernica* with a harlequin woman-cow reclining across it, holding a fan. Everywhere were tall tribal sculptures. The one near us seemed to grow out of a trunk or to have been made of a pulp of twiglike branches pressed together to form a dark porous substance: sticklike legs, bent, round thighs, a thick round penis with a hole at the center; a taut protruding belly that the figure appeared to be holding up with its arms, obscuring the chest, the head made of a hollow with a forehead hanging down and a wide nose with enormous nostrils carved into it. It had no eyes, only orbs. The Princess thought these pieces should have been in museums. Or that Hare should have given one to each of his friends. "He has weighed himself down with all this," she said.

At the center of the room, as downstairs, there was a conference of chairs, large and small ones, and they, too, rendered the human presence somehow accessory—possible but by no means necessary. It was the house of *res*—the thing—and things ruled it. Paintings communed among themselves; sculptures stalked the space; books everywhere infiltrated the territory: they were its true inhabitants. Words owned the Gloomy Castle, predated us and would outlive us. One *felt* it.

I asked the Princess to tell me about the dream of the ostrich, one of her recurring nightmares when she had been five years old. She dreamt she was in a bare room, standing against the wall; to the right of her, there was a small round drain in the floor; to the left, an open doorway with light streaming in from it. She waited in a state of anxiety, knowing the ostrich to be on its way. Soon, it appeared, walked across the room to the drain, bent its head on its tall neck to peck at invisible things in the drain. Then the Princess would wake up, shaking with fear. Because she had lived in the Tuscan Maremma till she was eight, she had never seen an ostrich in her life, had never been to a zoo, did not remember ever seeing an illustration of one. At the time of the nightmare, she did not even know that what she had seen was an ostrich, but it was one, exact in every detail.

Her other recurring nightmare was of a tall farm cart piled high with hay. It was about four times the size of a normal farm cart. On top of the hay would be sitting four or five bandits. This dream had a rational core at least: there had been bandits in the area where she had grown up. One of them had been hired by her uncle to keep other bandits off the estate. One day he came, said he wanted to give up his dishonest life, and handed her uncle his gun. Months later, he demanded his gun back, saying banditry was after all the only thing he knew.

The Princess and her brother were raised by a peasant woman, a *fattoressa* named Selide, "who had fine sentiments," the Princess said. Every night they slept in the same bed: Selide in the middle, the Princess on one side, and her brother on the other. Before she went to sleep, the Princess amused herself by watching the reflection of dancing flames from the fireplace on the ceiling and listening to the crackling of embers. In the morning from the window, they watched the oxen filing up in pairs to have the wooden yoke laid on their shoulders before heading out to the fields. At night, all the animals—oxen, donkeys, horses—came to drink at a long trough in front of the house. One bull was sickly and every afternoon they went to pay him a visit. Before the animals returned, the children would sometimes go jump up and down in the soft hay that had been prepared for the animals to sleep on in the haylofts.

"But that was before industrialization, and before the first and second wars," the Princess said. "What a disaster. But perhaps we are better off as we are, free of those thousands of acres of land and the responsibility of farming them." She liked visiting the countryside and admiring it from the window of a car but not the idea of living there.

Everyone rode horses. There was a narrow path from Bagno di Romagna to Viamaggio called the Bride's Jump, because there the entire cavalcade of a wedding cortège had leapt to its death into a ravine. The Princess's grandfather had later built a proper road over it.

Of all the estates her family had owned—seven of several thousand acres each—only two were left, Viamaggio and La Valentina. The oldest house, in the Apennines, above Sansepolcro, a building of the 1300s, had been forfeited by a cousin. The Princess said of him, "He was not content with farming the land and looking after the three thousand acres that were allotted to him. Out of some naïve ambition, he wanted to be a publisher. Another nobleman embroiled him in a venture to make a book that would be Italy's thanks to America for helping it to recover after the war. It was some consequence of the Marshall Plan. I asked him, 'Are you quite sure?' and he said, 'Of course—De Gasperi, the prime minister, is involved, too.' He went to Florence to supervise the project of which he was made chief executive officer. How so much money could have been spent producing a single book is a mystery, but he had to sell everything to defray his debts and after that he devoted himself to medicine. When he sold the house, he did so with everything in it, including the centuries-old library and every trace of the family's history, and he refused to discuss the subject ever again."

At the age of eight the Princess was sent to school in Rome, at first to a boarding school, then to a public school. There the nuns handed out prizes every week—a blue ribbon if one had been good, a yellow sash if one had been very good. She never got either until one day her father went to see the Mother Superior and mentioned that he had a relative high up in the Vatican. The following week the Princess was awarded a yellow sash.

Artichokes, hamburgers, spinach, and asparagus at the Gloomy Castle. By mistake we ordered a film that seemed slow even in fast forward. The Princess went to bed at midnight but a little while later the door of the elevator opened again and she beckoned to me. She said: the bleeding has started again—more of it this time. I wondered: was the treatment making her worse? She must have wondered, too.

Hare switched channels as though urgent news of the universe were being announced and he couldn't find where—his way of being despondent. I got up and went downstairs to the kitchen which the housekeeper Lupe had left all clean and quiet, the flame of the candle flickering on the seated child-saint, Niño de Atocha, and on the red carnations. It was the house of a solitary man, Hare, surrounded by solitary women. I sat at the little table covered with a plastic tablecloth beneath the fluorescent light sculpture that made my blue pen seem grey.

Upstairs in bed Hare read, "Doubt falls upon us like a calamity . . . it was in us and we were predestined to it," in a book by E. M. Cioran. I asked him about objects in the room: a table drawn by a schizophrenic with pots of flowers and ornaments flying around it; two pear-shaped objects that looked like bottles in a lit doorway which he explained were pigeons; holy water from a shaman he knew well in an ancient and soiled plastic bottle; two Dogon figures. The pictures in his room were all gifts, he said. Near his bed, a very small image of the Virgin of Guadalupe.

The Princess was in the kitchen the next morning, drinking black coffee, smoking a cigarette. No improvement: could I call the doctor? I tried: no answer in one place, busy in the other. I kept trying. She said, "I don't even have those . . ." I put on Hare's raincoat and went around the corner to buy pads—strawberry jam and marmalade, too, while I was at it—and when I returned, I asked Hare to leave a message for one of the Princess's doctors. I conveyed to him that she was anxious, feeling weak, had been insisting in the most uncharacteristic way that I call her doctor: "Where can he be? Do you think he went out? Would he be in the country?" And though I answered all her questions, she soon asked them again. For the second day in a row, she did not feel like going for a walk. But finally Hare found her doctor, who said, "There's nothing to worry about," and those were the very words she wanted to hear. No sooner had she heard them than she cheered up, became one who had nothing to worry about: "This has raised my crest," she said. Hare headed for the kitchen to cook some eggs, and she called cheerfully, "Wait for me, I'm just going to put on some makeup."

After the scrambled eggs and ice cream, we had been talking about slavery, when she said, "We are so lucky not to have been born to labor long hours under the sun."

The doctor decided that the Princess was to have a stronger dose of radiation to stem the bleeding. When I went to pick her up, she was saying she didn't think she should have another treatment but just see and be seen by her doctor's stand-in, the man with the lilac hair and sad eyes. Hare was firm: the chief doctor had insisted she should have the treatment.

As we left the house, Lupe said, *"Adios,"* and the Princess called gaily, *"Adios, caballero. . . .* There was a caballero at the beginning of *Don Quixote*—I never read it to the end."

We took a cab and while riding along she said, "It's funny, I had a cigarette earlier, and it made me feel weaker. Some things have a different effect with the radiation." As she always did, she asked me how my work was going. I mentioned the Greek fountain in Gallipoli and the story of the three nymphs that metamorphosed into streams—Biblis, Dirce, and Salmace. And she said, "Dirce was the name of my seamstress in Rome, before I started finding clothes at Givenchy. I heard about her in my last year of school through a friend. She was Tuscan, from Chianciano, and had a predilection for me. She would go to Paris and buy patterns from the best designers. The first thing she made for me was by Chanel—a navy blue crêpe-de-chine dress with a V neck in a shiny fabric." Later, when the Princess was married and unable to afford custom-made clothes, Dirce would let her have the original samples, once she was done with them, at a fraction of the cost.

The Princess took my arm getting out of the cab and we headed for the radiation center, into the inner waiting room. Every chair was taken: there was an eighteen-year-old with Hodgkin's disease accompanied by her mother, a young science teacher. They were Orthodox Jews, so her hair was shaved off and she wore a wig. She was bemoaning the fact that Lubavitch Jews were converting so many "colored" people. She had reprimanded her daughter on a previous visit for speaking about her illness, saying she would not find a husband by arranged marriage if it became known that she had cancer. A woman seated next to the young girl, also a teacher, of economics, urged her to go against her mother's judgment and speak to her friends, to be open about her illness. The economics teacher was having thirty radiation treatments on her breast. She was very tired: she taught in the morning, then at two-thirty left Rockland County and drove into the city. It was usually eight-thirty by the time she got home; she ate something, spent half an hour with her son, then went to sleep.

The Princess returned after her treatment and seemed in a better frame of mind. The nutritionist explained to her what jello was, and in the cab the Princess told me that fifty years earlier a doctor on Harley Street, in London, had prescribed that she make gelatin by simmering bones in water for about ten hours and then feed spoonfuls of the substance to her daughter who had a calcium deficiency. She was astounded that now one could make gelatin from a powder that came in an envelope all ready to be dissolved. After a pause she said, "I hope I can start to come here on my own soon. I don't like to disturb you." To console her, I said, "I don't have to do it, you know," and added, "We are not even related." She laughed.

She remembered suddenly the time President Clinton had come to Rome and made a speech, saying, "We are all one family." "That would not impress the Romans," she said. Her friend Ennio Flaiano, who wrote scripts for Fellini, in a play titled *The Continuously Interrupted Conversation,* in which a Martian lands in Rome, had a Roman paparazzo saying, "Move over, you Martian—you're in the way!"

The mint tea came and just then the phone rang and Hare, who had been peeling an apple in a spiral, picked it up and when he found the call was from his faraway lands, he vanished into the kitchen.

We ate bread in the kitchen, waiting for Hare to come down-stairs. "I don't know how he came to be called Hare," the Princess ruminated. "Perhaps one Easter: there are those Easter hares made of chocolate—he was always the hare." We opened a bottle of organic white wine. The Princess took a cautious sip and said, "Wine has to be first rate, or there is no point at all in drinking it." She had debated hav-ing a whiskey but decided against it. She thought cognac might be better if one was in danger of hemorrhaging.

The next day she came weakly into the conference of chairs in the big room at the Gloomy Castle where we sat with the philosopher who believed like the prophet-visionary Gioacchino da Fiore that we may already have entered the age of the spirit, only since the kingdom of the spirit was free, there was no way to be sure. The philosopher was an optimist. Beneath Hare's inability to be easily stirred was optimism.

We all had seven oleous drops of a regenerative herbal substance for the flu as a cocktail, and the philosopher spoke of his disgust for cockroaches which had driven him to change houses in L.A. three or four times. The Princess was uncommonly silent and only at the table, over arti-chokes, chicken cutlets, broccoli, carrots, asparagus, uttered a line of conversation here and there. I felt the quaking of the philosopher, the quaking of the Princess, the quaking of Hare—tired spirits that day—and I felt strong by comparison.

During a break in a conference Hare had organized, the Princess said, "I have a fondness for minimalists: at least they do nothing." For hours, as lecturers spoke, she embodied the aristocratic ideal of equanimity. She sat upright and did not stir. Only towards the end of three hours did I notice a slight shifting in her seat. She said, "If I find the person who designed this chair, I'll throw it in his face." When the architect read a litany about the house, ending with a litany on death, she became indignant. "Everyone wants to write poems and novels. It's a great pity."

The historian listed all the different ways that treason had been punished since the beginning of time: in one instance, the traitor was disemboweled to expose the very place where treason was thought to form; in another, the body of the traitor was quartered and each quarter was sent to the four borders in the four directions.

The specialist of voodoo approved of anything that would constitute treason. His kind of astrology, he said, was the kind where one told the stars what to do. No language is superior, no language is inferior, transcend yourself, he concluded, and showed a black-and-white slide of a woman whose eyes were "bursting with the coming of the spirit."

Having my limbs waxed by Emma, who is Puerto Rican. "Did I tell you?" Emma said. "Did I tell you about my son? When were you here the last time?" No, I replied, she hadn't told me about her son. "He died," she said, and threw her arms around me. "Thirty-nine years old. He had a heart attack." Emma spread honey wax on a patch of my legs, then laid a piece of cloth over it and pulled the hair off. As she did so, meticulously, she told me how it had happened, every now and then wiping away the tears. Emma's eyes and my legs were receiving the same tender attention. "My daughter-in-law called seven times, but every time I answered, she did not want to tell me. She waited till someone else answered the phone. The phone rang and rang, and every time there was no one on the other end. My husband said, 'They hear your voice, and they know they got the wrong number, they hang up.' That day was a Saturday. My son was coming to see me the next day for five days. I was waiting for him. I went to work that Saturday. One of my clients was hysterical while I was doing her nails. She was crying. 'What's the matter?' I asked her. She said, 'My son died of a heart attack.' I was crying, too, I was so sad. All that day I was sad afterwards. When I got home, my husband said, 'If you had to cry like that for every person who dies—and by the way call Julio.' I hadn't heard from him that day. My other son, José, had gone to a

Yankee game—he lives with me. I didn't feel like cooking,
so I didn't. We just stayed home. I was so sad, I didn't feel
like eating, and the phone kept ringing. At ten o'clock I
heard knocking on the door. I heard my nephew's voice, 'It's
me, open the door.' I opened. He said, 'You're going to have
to be strong,' and I see my sister behind the door crying hysterical. I said, 'Something happened to my Julio. He died.
Something happened to him?'" Emma was spreading hard
wax to remove the hair along what is known as the bikini
line. She had a system: she slipped a strip of cloth, like those
she used to pull off the wax, beneath the front of the
panties, then tied the two ends together so that the outer
edge of the hair was uncovered. It was as she did this that
she told me the culmination of the story: "'No,' they said,
'it's Julio. He had a car accident, he died.' I thought at first
that he died of the car accident. I thought I would not be
able to recognize him, but he died of a heart attack. He
looked beautiful there in the casket—his beard trimmed, his
mustache trimmed—you see he was coming to New York
to see me, so he had been to the barber. He was a beautiful man, inside and outside. Three weeks before, I was in
Puerto Rico, and he took me to the beach. He worked at an
airline, so every five weeks or so he came or I went. The
mother of a cousin had died. My son, he took me aside, and
he said, 'Mother, promise not to be angry, but I have to tell
you something.' I said, 'I'm not giving you any money': it
was a joke we had between us. He said, 'Mama, I want to
die before you.' My daughter-in-law told me he always told
her, 'I don't know what I am going to do if I have to bury
my mother.' He used to call me here at work, and a few
minutes later he would call again. They would say, 'It's your

son, he says he forgot to tell you something.' I would go to the telephone, and he would say, 'I forgot to tell you how much I love you.' He always said he loved his mother first, then his children. His father, my first husband, was at the grave the other day, my sister saw him. He was at the grave crying, crying. I want to go back, but I am not strong enough yet. I'm gonna wait. But then I want my son here. My daughter-in-law wanted to cremate him, but my first husband said, 'Please, I pay for the burial and the funeral, but let me do it our way.' We are Christian. I want to take him back here. He loved New York. He didn't want to be in Puerto Rico, but his family was there. Anyway his wife is a beautiful woman. Two years from now she will want to make a new life for herself. I want to bring my son back here to be with me. My son José wants that, too." Emma rubbed my legs and arms with oil to remove the bits of wax, then she said, "I'm sorry—I gave you all my sadness."

On my way home I ran into the widow of the writer. She recounted the death of their favorite pug. Her husband's secretary had dropped him while playing with him. He had broken a leg and a hip. The leg had been mended right away, but the broken hip was only discovered later. He had also done some other injury to himself for which he had to be operated on in New York. The animal clinic charged thirty-eight thousand dollars to nurse him. The operation went well, but two weeks later he wouldn't eat, then he started coughing. It was eleven at night. She picked him up to take him to the doctor, but he was already dead by the time she arrived. She felt his weight change in her arms, and that's how she knew he had died. When he died, she said her husband's health went into a decline, he had loved that dog so much. She had her husband's ashes and the pug's, and she was going to bury them together. It used to cost one hundred and seventy dollars to have the young pug, who had inherited the elder pug's medals, washed at the vet's.

She told me, when you worked at the designer's, you helped me buy clothes I still wear to this day—twice a year I go to the showroom and get some things, always the same sorts of things.

The Princess was pleased to see me. She said: "I used to think solitude was beatitude, and now it is all subverted; I used to thrill to an hour by myself. But then I was never by myself."

On the table in the midst of the conference of jackets, there was a bear's face made from half a coconut shell, a little brown bear and a devil bear with horns on its head in a plastic dome that could be seen through a flurry of silver and gold confetti when turned upside down. "It is part of Hare's collection of bears," the Princess said, "of which I am one." She delivered the line deadpan, as usual, then continued gravely, "A mother at the school Hare went to once asked me, 'You wouldn't be a bit bearish, would you?'" The Princess had refused all invitations to appear at the school, not wanting to be dragged into an inescapable cycle of niceties with people she cared nothing about.

When he was four, Hare had to have his shoes custom made by a shoemaker on Via Rasella. To be precise, they were lace-up boots, with an inset to arch the sole of his feet. On the day of his fitting, the Princess took him by the hand, and they made their way down the steep incline of Via Capo le Case. Suddenly a terrible explosion was heard, and Hare remembers that the Princess instantly turned back. A convoy of German soldiers had been blown up by a faction of the resistance: it was the famous incident of Via

Rasella, for which the Nazis retaliated by killing three hundred and fifty at the Fosse Ardeatine, three for every one of theirs, as they promised they would if the culprits didn't come forward.

"What is to become of me? I see my future as very dim, like a nebula," said the Princess, sitting at the little table in the kitchen as Hare spoke on the phone. I pulled up a pinkish stool and sat by her.

She calculated that her treatment would be over by the sixth of December. "How long will it take me to recover?" she asked. "Will I be well enough to return to Rome?" I think that she was eager to go home, to be free once again. Given her weakness since the radiation, the Princess could not go out unless someone went with her. Ruy was the only person with whom she could come and go as she pleased, feeling in command of her movements to a degree, but Ruy was leaving the next day, and then I would be the only one outside the castle to take her out. I am sure she dwelt on all this, on her increasing dependence.

We went to Three Guys, and she had fish souvlaki, Hare had shrimp Corfu, I had California cobb salad with Russian dressing. It was noisy there. Hare sat looking out onto the street, the Princess and I at the kitchen and the throngs of diners. Hare was adamant that the Princess should have fish, though she was not remotely in the mood for it.

Ruy had another night with some Russian friends and met one at the top of a golden skyscraper who told him, "Teaching is one thing, life is another." Then when Ruy was leaving, he said to him, "If you ever want women, Russian or not Russian, I can get you some."

I told the Princess the story. She was grave and said the Russian was not someone one should frequent. She found nothing funny in the story. She smelt danger, and it was to be kept at a distance.

Hare arrived, bustling. It was time to go for the radiation treatment. He went to put on his coat. She went to put on hers. Can we drop you off? the Princess asked. Hare said that one should walk. He was uncharacteristically stern. I saw them into a cab and set off. Later he came to dinner: roast, broccoli rabe, potatoes with parsley, chocolate ice cream. I lit a fire, asked him why he had been so nervous. Nothing, he said, just that he had a headache. He brought pink roses on long stems: Hare, happy in my domain.

Lupe said when I arrived at the castle the next day: "I was just thinking, 'I wonder where the señorita is,' when I caught sight of you through the kitchen window, which means you will live long." Hare was cheerful, maybe because Moon was arriving that day. Sole, spinach and asparagus, cauliflower, ice cream, and the apple tarts that the Princess liked so well. I brought her vermillion-pink carnations. The mention of Thanksgiving, about which she said only that she hoped it would be over with soon, made her think of the feast of La Befana, the Witch, in Rome, when people dip their brooms in the fountains and splash passersby.

We talked of Ruy and how he took certain stories Hare

had told him and told them about himself. For instance, I said, the story about your husband saying he might never have married if he hadn't met you. The Princess said, "My husband said that? It's the first I hear of it." Hare confirmed his father's statement. She seemed neither pleased nor displeased, just mildly surprised.

She had been to the salon across the street that morning, and there was a sparkling new layer of mother-of-pearl varnish on her nails. The hairdresser had cut her hair very carefully, "one hair at a time," she said, because there were no other customers. She was worried about running out of foundation cream. One store she went to didn't have any and she was quite determined to go to Bloomingdale's after the radiation if it hadn't been that the machine had broken in the course of the day and she was called for her treatment an hour and a half after her appointment. We sat in the pink waiting room, and I took down the name of the makeup: Re-Nutriv, Polished Beige makeup creme.

Waiting with us were almost ten people, including the Orthodox Jewish young woman who looked to be no more than twenty, wearing her wig. One woman who was there every day asked her, "Is it true that in your religion if someone is mortally ill, you change their name so that the angel of death might get confused and go elsewhere?" The woman replied, smiling, "Yes, it's true, but only if they are very ill." Her father, in black velvet yarmulke, nodded and said it was a long ceremony and usually the invalid's name was changed to Haim. The women discussed the benefits of aloe cream to soothe the burn of radiation on their chest; one maintained it had done nothing for her and she was now using antibiotic cream. The economics teacher I had first seen a few days earlier said they recommended wearing nothing around the house, and she said, "Now wouldn't that be nice around my fifteen-year-old son?"

The Princess looked more elegant and energetic than any of the other patients. She went to change, and when she returned, wearing the hospital gown and with it, her veiled stockings, blue suede shoes, a hand-tied bow, blue sweater, little Givenchy purse, and large plastic pearls, looked ravishingly elegant. Small pearl necklaces, real ones, like the one she had that were once her mother's, did not adorn, she said. Perhaps she should sell it—someone had told her it was worth a fortune. Hare had given her some silver necklaces from Mexico, but she never wore them. The emerald on the ring finger of her right hand had belonged to her mother and been mounted by Bulgari with diamonds. There was a diadem in a safe-deposit box, too—utterly useless, she said, but it had been in the family for many generations, and if she did not take care of it, she knew of no one who would. She had once had rubies and a sapphire from Kashmir, but they had been stolen.

The Princess said, "Will you be here while Hare is gone?" I said yes, of course. Leaving the radiation center, she said, "Moon is coming. How annoying that we cannot all be together since Hare hasn't told him about you yet." But then we agreed that a family united sounded better than it was. "Individual relationships are the most important," she said.

Suddenly, through the french door, a shower of golden ginkgo leaves was blown off the branches by a gust of wind, falling in a swirling profusion. The table, the ground, the white wire chairs were covered with a thick billowy layer of them. Hare named it Desolation Garden, because the ginkgo leaves had poisoned the earth and only strange willful shrubs seemed to want to grow there. I minded the ginkgo trees in the summer because they blocked the sun, but now their fallen leaves made up for that by gathering up every drop of light and reflecting it. They were green, then yellow, dull gold, and bright gold as the light changed. At half past four, the sky was leaden and the leaves never brighter.

The Princess had already had ten treatments. Only seven left to go. She told the nurse that she had a dinner engagement and she was put on the machine immediately so that in fifteen minutes we were ready to leave. It was too early to go to the sculptor's opening, she said. She would not be the "cretin," as she put it, and be the first to arrive. We sat in the reception area of the radiation center and waited for what she deemed a decent hour to leave. We arrived at twenty to seven and the gallery was already quite full. Of one piece—a bust suspended over a disk, one long arm stretched through a hoop and swooping down till the hand rested on a rectangular bronze slab resembling a tomb-

stone—she said, "making horns," for superstition because
it was such an ominous-looking object, that she liked it. She
scrutinized every piece minutely—the polyplike white marble glob on the ground with leakings at the back; the giant
black cube; the white plaster and cardboard unicorn with a
mute mulish faceless face; the blue skeleton crate; the yellow canoe. She observed the guests, drank a glass of white
wine from a plastic glass, kept her coat on. It was soon
seven-thirty.

When Hare came, she mumbled she was not going to the
dinner, and he scolded her, saying she had told the sculptor
she would go, and now she would have to do so. Chas-
tened, she said she was quite resigned to not going. Hare
walked ahead, then hailed a cab. In the backseat, the tension was palpable. I tried to touch Hare's knee, as though
by so doing I could dispel his rage. He looked out the window of the cab. The Princess, recovering some of her poise,
prattled on about the lights of the city.

At Fifty-seventh Street, the traffic came to a halt in front
of the Trump building. The sun was setting. An ambulance
stood, its back doors open, revealing a brightly lit interior
with a crisply sheeted stretcher. A small crowd of onlookers
hung around blankly in the gathering dusk. The cause of all
the commotion was a black woman standing naked, her left
arm around her waist, her right propped up on it, the chin
resting delicately on a curved index finger. The grace of
her pose made her nakedness not seem out of place. She
appeared to be scrutinizing the building's directory—white
plastic letters on black felt, framed in the standard Trump
gold. She must have been in her fifties; a high inclined forehead, a long Egyptian nose; her hair cut short to the scalp,

long limbs, a woman's belly. An orderly stepped down from the ambulance, took a few steps towards her and threw a white sheet over her. As though she had been draped in a ceremonial mantle, the woman held the sheet carelessly in place with one arm, a chieftain surrounded by her subjects. She seemed unconscious of the people staring at her—her own eyes were fixed on an internal screen—and next to her impassive majesty they appeared awkward. She swept unaided into the waiting ambulance, her glittering carriage, and our cab edged on. The scene had to be described to the Princess, who had seen only a blur.

At the Turkish restaurant, dinner had already started. The sculptor and another man got up to give us their seats at the table. I felt we should leave but somehow stuck it out through the hors d'oeuvres, then salad, grilled meats, white rice. The Turkish musicians played, and at first one heard only a din. A woman got up and began to dance gracefully to the rhythm. All of a sudden, another, very tall, thin woman in a black miniskirt and clinging black-and-white sweater got up on a chair and moved her hips slowly, as though to announce the beginning of her dance. She stepped down from the chair and came to stand in front of the musicians. Her arms were up above her head, and she moved her hips up and down, shifting her feet inches forwards and backwards. Then she brought her hands to her groin and made a triangle with her fingers around it, gathering the fingers up and down the middle of her body. She went up to the raven-haired, mustachioed saxophone player and jiggled her belly in front of the mouth of his instrument. Her eyes were open, concentrated on a place within and serene, the lips slightly smiling. It was a look of abandon, delicately erotic. Hare was very struck by her "gift," as he called it, and was indignant when the sculptor went over to ask her to dance again; he said that what she had done was perfect and that it was not fair to ask for more. But she acquiesced to the request and came back, this time going up to the drum player and jiggling her hips right near where his hands were beating the skin of the drum. Her presence heated up the room. Many smoked. The Princess said gleefully, "We will all land in jail, I can feel it in my bones." The sculptor came to her chair and knelt by her side. She caressed his cheek; he held her hand and held it the entire time he knelt and talked to her for about ten minutes— I heard only "the love of a parent" and understood: she loved the sculptor.

Nearly everyone got up and danced to the Turkish music, with its plucked, shivering strings, low-voiced moaning songs, some knowing what to do, others doing their best. Guests at other tables began to spin their white napkins round and round above their heads. The Princess picked up her napkin and spun it energetically above her head longer than almost anyone, egged on by the African artist across the table from her, who had smiled admiringly at her from the start, seeing her smoke and drink two chilled anisettes straight up.

When we dropped her off at the castle, she said intellectuals were never any good at dancing and that one had to have navy officers for that. Hare said his father never danced. When I asked her who those navy officers were, she replied enigmatically that she could always find one to dance with. We left her and went home, into the crackling air of falling icy snow, and the next day the last of the pink roses were laden with it. I shook it off, cut the roses at the end of their stem, and put them in a tall glass vase, salvaging the last shreds of fall.

I knew that the Princess was tired whenever I saw her walking with a prancing step: she lifted her feet up more than usual and walked as though on eggs. She was making an effort to appear energetic. That evening, in the lobby of the building where we left the sculptor, after seeing his show again, she shook his hand and walked away without slipping her hand under my arm as she did normally, so that in case he might be watching she would not appear to need any help.

In the following days, she had the remaining doses of radiation, ending the day before Hare left for Mexico. On that visit to the hospital, one of the patients had left a fragment of the newspaper on his seat and I borrowed it to read about the Chinese announcing they had found the reincarnation of the Panchen Lama, although the Dalai Lama had already some time before announced finding that same reincarnation in a six-year-old. Beijing's candidate was also six. The Chinese government declared the Tibetan's a fraud and his parents two dishonest individuals seeking self-aggrandizement. The Princess said, "All this is strictly for the bonzes: Buddhism, immanence—I prefer Immanuel Kant."

As we left the hospital, she sighed, "There won't even be the radiations anymore." It was at least something for her to do and it guaranteed her an hour or so of company every day of the week except for the weekend. "But we can do things, can't we?" she asked. Before leaving for Mexico, Hare brought a dozen irises, and I still had pink carnations from the last time he had brought me flowers, and the last two pink roses from the terrace.

One summer visiting the country estate of the writer Luigi Barzini, the Princess, who was then in her forties, contracted Q fever, so named because it came from Queensland, Australia, transported by cattle: she got it from a mosquito bite. In the kitchen she told me: "I heard that they have discovered a new virus even more virulent than AIDS." She puffed on her cigarette.

I said I was glad she would be staying for Christmas. She said, "Am I? I don't know anything. I am so confused I need a psychiatrist." She wailed comically. "Hare has been in a terrible mood," she added.

She remembered her first Christmas tree when she was six in San Donato, the smell of pine, all the presents beneath it. Her father bought the same sort of gifts for his children as for the bailiff's children, Guido and Nanni. The Princess had met Guido sixty years later, running a restaurant not far from San Donato, and he had almost fainted with joy at seeing her again.

At dinner—Hare cooked steaks, and Lupe asparagus, spinach, and broccoli—the Princess remembered that she had gone to see John Gielgud at the Old Vic in seven different productions of *Hamlet*, the last on July 19, 1939, before she and her husband left for Italy, right before the war. The costumes had already been packed off to Denmark, so the actors wore contemporary clothes. Her husband hardly ever went with her to the theatre on the pretext that having written a book on the English theatre, he knew too much about it and that he had seen everything there was to see. She had often waited on long lines to buy tickets.

After the war, at the club Capannina in Forte dei Marmi— not the elegant one, the Princess specified, the popular one—she and a friend had met two burly Englishmen who were there for a holiday. They had asked her and her friend to dance many times in the course of that one evening. Her husband thought they must be greengrocers; he was probably jealous of their surprising agility. There was an admiral once who wanted to give a party in her honor on his boat, which was moored in the harbor of La Spezia, but that had seemed too compromising to her and she had declined.

I went to pick up the Princess at the castle. We were invited to lunch with my father and uncle. In the taxi, she spoke of Jupiter. A satellite had been programmed to study Jupiter, then die, but first it had ejected a piece that had returned to Earth with all the information. Soon we would find out, she said. It was a planet made of gases that caused constant eruptions. "It is a tiny fragment of the universe," she said, "just as New York is." After a while she added, "But what do we care?"

"The dollar is strong," she said, "and the lira holds because it hinges on the dollar. Let's hope the franc holds up in spite of all the strikes." She asked for a scotch and I noticed she drank very little of it. But she sat at the table and made conversation with my father about Jupiter. My uncle said that it had been scientifically proven that women had existed long before men. "Which came first?" she pondered. I said, "Woman, the egg, then man who is the chicken." "Man, the chicken," she repeated, delighted.

After lunch we stood in the middle of the room and my father said we looked as though we were going to do a *benim:* "Thirteen people huddle together and recite it." "Eleven," my uncle rectified. "Eleven men," his wife amended. "I couldn't even go to temple and read the prayer when my parents died because a woman is not allowed to do that."

The Princess said, "That's good, very good—it leaves us free to do as we wish!" I sat next to her. She remembered a certain Count Cantoni who had materialized in the course of one of her dancing lessons at the Scuola Pichetti in Rome. He wore a black cape, lined in satin. He swept it off, waved away the young man who had been dancing with the Princess and took over, singing a melancholic song to a mimosa as he did so. She was fourteen years old. When the dance ended, he bowed and vanished.

We talked of Christmas presents and I said Hare had told me that on Christmas Eve he and his brother always waited impatiently to see when their mother would go out to buy them presents; she would hold out till the very last minute so that sometimes they wondered whether the stores would even be open. "Naturally," she said, "we would go by a toy store and they would point to one thing and another and I told them, 'Certainly not, better put it right out of your mind!' Horrible things." Still, children had a fascination with gifts, I told her. "Only when they are not properly trained," she said. "And now," she added brightly, "I read in *Scientific American* that terrorists already have nuclear weapons at their disposal, so they could end up in children's hands, too."

I told her I had stumbled onto a mysterious Swedish church on Fifty-third Street that seemed so quiet in the chaos of midtown and she asked, "Is it heated?" I said yes. She asked impishly, "And can one smoke there?"

She disparaged all the Christmas preparations—the purchase of a tree, the dragging of it indoors, the decoration of it, wrapping gifts, distributing them. Hare asked me to let the Princess know he would like a red scarf from her. Years ago, she had given him one and he had worn it so much, it had lost both its color and shape. I found a red scarf of the correct shade and length in an Indian store and bought it. She gave me the twenty-five dollars it cost and then instructed me on the packing: brown paper and string. She was thrilled when she saw the package that I had followed her request to the letter. Hare said she was happy with her gifts, that her disdain for Christmas was simply a matter of style: one could not be seen to lend countenance to such sentimentalisms.

I saw Hare's daughter in the midst of a dozen other people at the painter's Christmas party. She was dressed in white, and we were not introduced. I spoke to her not at all until the very end of the evening and then only because she happened to be sitting nearby as I looked at the Neapolitan nativity scene in the fireplace, with four "sleepers," the three Wise Men moving towards the grotto, an incongruous

Cuban soldier, merchants of all varieties selling salame and fish, chickens and pigs. She looked at me intently and smiled once or twice, and I liked her as one might take a liking to someone new at a dinner. No abstractions to ruin the spontaneity of that first meeting. We had met before when she was a baby, the first time, a child the second and third times. I presumed that she did not remember any of them.

The Princess asked to see the Pergamon marbles at the Metropolitan Museum. There were two warriors, one upside down, falling over a horse, of which only the head was visible. I read to her some of the mythological tales: Prometheus was punished by Zeus for bringing fire to Earth and condemned to having an eagle eat his liver all day long; then during the night the liver reformed, only to be eaten again the next day. Heracles arrived and shot an arrow through the eagle, freeing Prometheus from his torment. The Princess looked up at the rounded face of a young athlete and said, "Classical sculptures had a great deal of expression, not like neoclassical ones, with their empty faces. Life is in them." She looked hard and long, then sat recovering for a while.

At the treehouse, the Princess asked to hear Benedetti Michelangeli, as she always did whenever she came. "Prophetic soul," she said when I brought her an ashtray before she had asked for one.

She was distraught to be told that she had to have four more doses of radiation. They did not explain, and she only found out when she went for the first one that it was yet another kind of treatment from any she'd had before:

instruments were inserted deep into her womb and she was asked to breathe deeply so as to lessen the pain; the radiation itself lasted seven minutes. "I am infuriated with myself," she told me after the visit with her chief oncologist and the news that her return to Rome would once again be postponed for almost a month. Spaghetti with rabe. She spoke of the sculptor: he surfaced in her conversation as though he were someone she lived with, and she did live with him, mentally.

At the castle that evening, she asked to see the Russian film version of "Lady with a Lapdog" by Chekhov. It was in Russian with English subtitles that she could hardly keep up with, given her failing eyesight. After twenty minutes she murmured, "Too many conversations," and started talking to me. She preferred Clinton to the Kennedys because she thought the Kennedys all had crooked faces. She recounted to me the play by Gogol called *The Marriage,* in which a hardened bachelor who has finally succumbed to the schemes of a matchmaking friend—one who envies his freedom—at first extols marriage, "real bliss, the sort of bliss you find only in fairy tales." Then, as the wedding is about to be celebrated and the guests and his bride-to-be have gathered downstairs, he is suddenly chilled by the finality of tying himself up "just like that, for the rest of your life, for ever and ever. . . ." He can't think what to do, but then catches sight of an open window and, setting caution and propriety aside, leaps out of it to the ground below and a waiting cab.

The fire was crackling; the Princess sat on the white couch wearing her blue Givenchy dress, green sweater with gold buttons, and thick blue cardigan over everything, as she felt the cold. She lit a cigarette and said, "For nearly seventy years, the Soviet Union and America were uncontested world leaders and what did they do with all the power? Nothing. They couldn't even get rid of the untouchables in India."

Hare had left for Houston that morning and when I went to pick her up, she was feeling particularly anxious. She had eaten an egg for breakfast, she told me, hoping it would give her energy but it had not had the desired effect. To the unaccompanied cello suites of Bach, played by Yo-Yo Ma, the Princess nodded off on the couch again, as she had done a few days earlier. Her skeleton was triumphing over flesh. One hand propping up her head, the Princess made a grimace as she slept that raised her upper lip into a terrible scowl, a violence of emotion she never consciously expressed. I noticed the sadness of her mouth and that the eyes were deeply shaded. When she opened them some moments later, she said, "Socrates wrote a book in praise of old age. I never read it, but perhaps I should to find out what he thought was so wonderful about it. Perhaps we missed something." Again she said "we," including me in her old age.

I thought that she was being killed along with the tumor

or that she had finally sided with the tumor and they would leave the world together. I made her a frittata with zucchini and tomatoes, and between us we finished a loaf of bread.

Sometimes, during the brief respites between my interludes with the Princess, I thought how one small act of kindness after another had led me out of my previous existence into this half-family life. In the first months, I would see the Princess then be eager to go home and fall back into my work, conversations with friends, and solitude. Then, little by little, the figure of the Princess, who had entered the stage surreptitiously, saying few lines, grew until what had been central characters and actions all were pushed to the sidelines and her voice and moods were all that was heard.

There were days when I was dismayed at the invasion. I had invited, even welcomed, the Princess into the enclave of secrecy that Hare and I had enveloped ourselves in. But I had never meant her to become a fixture. Her continued presence, day after day, created a skip in sequence, a crack in the road we were constantly afraid of falling into.

Hare found black-and-white photographs of his mother in an envelope marked "London." She posed very formally in each one, never smiling, in her impeccable outfits: tailleurs made of chiné wool and coats with fur trim, little snug hats set at an angle, those features that seemed etched, and the unsmiling mouth. The eyes had dark circles all around them. There was an absence about her, a detailed mirthlessness all the more surprising since in person she so liked to amuse and be amused. But to look at those photographed eyes calling from the midst of all the fashionable coordinated impeccabilities of cloth, cut, and shade was to see no one there, a physical body without the person. Could you accuse someone of absence? Was it a human failing? Or was it the failing of one not consistently on the earth and so, in some way, inhuman? That was a criticism leveled at the insensitive, the cruel, the selfish—that they were inhuman. An animal might eat you to stay alive: one did not blame the animal. An animal ignored your presence: one did not fault the animal. An animal neglected your needs: that was how an animal was. But an animal did not neglect its own needs. She took care of herself physically but her brain, that marvel of unblinking memory, quickness, analytical ability, she had kept, like a very large and dangerous dog, tethered, giving it no exercise, never letting it run, never letting it free, never giving it the possibility of feeling its own power. She had kept it to amuse, to repress and impress—the functions of an average brain—not hers.

The family was like a matinee performance six days a week. To see a person every day, whether they know or agree to be scrutinized or not. To see them again before they have had a chance to reform anecdotes and enthusiasm for the outside world, whether their store of faith, hope, and charity has had time to be replenished or not. Whether they have had time to remember they love or not. A jewel can bear to be looked at twenty-four hours a day and lose none of its beauty. A spirit inside a human body, bright as it may be, is always buried under layers of humors.

Hare brought crocuses one day; white and red carnations the next, to last till his return. Write to me, I told Hare, when he complained of not being able to send me a fax on the spur of the moment. I liked letters, envelopes, and stamps. You are a fetishist, he said. I agreed and said I was a fetishist even in the fact that I liked his spirit inside his body—we are all fetishists, or we would be content with a spirit in a box or simply with the air around us. My life, for so long, was a voice issuing from a receiver. My life with Hare was that. If the awkwardness of being with him in the space he inhabited normally, his *here,* made me feel the chasm with which family protected itself from family, all I needed to do was go home and wait for him to telephone and, when he did, to know that all the intimacy was there, and mine, as long as I remained the person elsewhere and did not melt into his everyday.

The Princess called. She had started taking a daily potion of herbs containing seaweed and felt stronger. She was in command of her body once more, ready for the next decade.

The collar of her blue jersey dress was laced with pink face powder. She could not see it, or that she had taken to putting too much pink rouge on her creased cheeks. I did not tell her because to cross the line into the realm of her person was to say that she was unable to gauge for herself.

Her oncologist visited her and found a lesion to which he applied some cream. It seemed a laughable remedy. The tumorous mass, he said, was now eighty-five percent cured. What about the remaining fifteen percent? She was to have two more radiations before her departure, and then the radiation would continue to do its work, eliminating malignant cells. When she returned to the waiting room, there was blood on her hospital gown.

I asked the Princess whether she wanted to sit down a moment to rest and she replied firmly, "I want to go home *now*. I've had enough of all this—*basta*. There are so many anesthetics, why can't they use them?" She may have been stoical, but she had reached her limit: "All that rubbish about natural childbirth is so vulgar. I had anesthetics for the birth of every one of my three children. Being born is not so pleasant for the child either—a little anesthetic is good for the baby, too." Did she have an epidural? No, she said, something that made her sleep quite peacefully. It sounded like total anesthesia. Hare found it hard to wake up in the morning. He lay in bed and looked ahead, as though waiting for the cells in his body to cooperate with the intention to get up.

The doctor said she wouldn't need another treatment a week later, only a checkup. But on the following Monday, after another checkup, he decided she should have one more after all. Walking to the dressing room, the Princess left two drops of blood in her wake, perfectly round and vermillion—a young girl's blood, just as the doctor had said on being told of her hemoglobin count, which was 13.50. He couldn't believe it could be so high after so much radiation, that she was not in the least bit anemic. It was clear he thought she was a human phenomenon in both mind and spirit, not one cell of her willing to concede defeat or to relinquish life. It was hard to see how she would ever die, not because she did not understand the inevitability of death but because she did not apply its powers to herself.

She took her own immortality for granted though her body was failing.

Edie, the nurse, said, "Can you get her panties for her?" I felt like a thief opening the Princess's locker without her leave, but it was preferable to asking her out loud. Inside, on the shelf, were the pantyhose she had removed—milky nylon still containing the curves of her limbs in air, folded in an ethereal mound like a caterpillar's discarded skin. The Givenchy blue jersey dress hung on a hanger, the black handbag was placed next to the pantyhose. I saw no panties and shut the locker.

Holding out a pad, Edie said to her, "Can you put this between your legs?" The Princess took the object with a swift delicate gesture, and when she reemerged, did a little dance in the doorway before proceeding to the toilet. We waited for the radiation machine to be repositioned for her. The Princess said Neapolitans believe one should hide well-being from the Almighty or it will attract his attention and he will cause trouble. In the waiting room, we listened to what other patients were saying. The Princess's condition seemed bright by comparison. One woman shook her head and muttered, "God knows, God shows." The Princess shrugged at what she termed the naïveté of Americans and asked me for a detailed explanation of the *Columbo* episode we had seen the night before on television.

A woman who is a sexual therapist finds her plane to Chicago is delayed till the next day and she returns to her office to pick up something she has forgotten. There, she surprises her husband making love to her secretary in the room patients use to have therapeutic sex in. The room is luridly decorated to incite the couples, with pearly lampshades and velvets, and the bed is made up with red satin sheets. She withdraws before he can see her, and while in Chicago, forms a plan to kill him. On her return, he picks her up at the airport. She asks him to meet her at the bar of the opera, next door to a reception she must attend. She goes to it, bringing with her a change of clothes, and vanishes into the ladies' room. She reemerges wearing a low-cut, clinging black dress, black stockings, high heels, a black wig, and a black hat. She heads for the bar, makes sure the bartender identifies her as a prostitute, and pretends to wait for a lover. When her husband arrives, though he recognizes her, he goes along with her game. She leads him to the sex therapy room at the office and he is so taken by her act that he does not see her retrieve a small revolver from her purse. She shoots him, then returns to the reception. A man follows her to the door of the bathroom where she changes back into herself. The man waits in vain for the woman in black to come out, but of course "she" never does. When the murder is investigated, this piece of evidence pointing to her disguise is her undoing.

The floor of the waiting room was spat-on linoleum, light grey with darker grey flecks, and at regular intervals a diamond-on-taupe linoleum. The chairs lining three walls were wood framed and attached to a base ring, like sleds, the seats covered by a beige wide-weave upholstery. The plastic wall covering was pink with grey, white, and orange drippings. There were two kinds of robes available—white with blue trims or white with small blue and yellow squiggles. The Princess always chose the second and, as she waited, wore over it her bright green sweater with gold buttons untarnished by wear. A sign above the stack of clean folded robes read: "For radiation safety and privacy reasons, please do not enter the technical area until you are called."

Our life together had become one of waiting rooms: I waited with her, waited for her, and all the while, too, waited for Hare—to call, to appear. She and I waited for the "treatment" to begin and to end, waited for the cure, waited unwittingly for things to improve, for an effect.

When one was in the throes of an illness, one's life, far from taking a vertiginous pace, slowed down almost un-bearably. It was like having driven a bicycle over a path that had unceremoniously landed one in a murky lake: one sank so slowly that there was ample time to observe every bub-ble, every weed. The rhythm of illness could not be rushed any more than it could be stayed.

During the "treatment" the Princess's body was no longer hers—it belonged to the illness and to the cure. "Take her to the bathroom and clean her up a little," the nurse said after one of the last and bloodier radiations. The idea of "cleaning her up a little" was preposterous, because the Princess had in no way relinquished care of her body. That would come much later.

We waited, and the Princess recalled the time her husband had attended a conference in Stresa for a firm called Monte-catini and she had gone off to see their stockings factory—one large room with a single attendant, a vast iridescent veil of nylon from which the stockings proceeded at the end of the assembly. The stockings were of very bad quality, she said, and ran almost as soon as she put them on. She had gone with her younger son, who must have been in his teens. They visited the botanical gardens of Villa Taranto, and the lake where she had almost drowned once at the age of eighteen. She had gone to visit relatives who had a house on its shores and tobogganed down a slide into the water. The toboggan would normally have released her as she was about to enter the water, but that time it didn't, and she felt herself sinking into the still murky water. She wasn't scared. "Strange," she said. A lifeguard had come to her rescue.

Another time she had gone to see the Etruscan tombs at Tarquinia with Ezra Pound, walking down the steps supporting him, afraid he would fall because "he was so tall," she said, and always suffered from backache. She said that he had stopped talking after his internment at St. Elizabeth's Hospital, it had been such a terrible blow.

Of another writer she had known, she said, "If Leo had been alive, he would still be writing by hand." I said I thought he would be using a computer. "I am certain," she said, "that there must be *some* people who still write by hand." She implied, superior people, who had no use for "machines," as she called them. I asked whether she meant computers or typewriters. She stalled, then said, "Either one." Oddly enough, her husband had written for sixty years almost exclusively on an Olivetti but she had often objected to the noise. The Princess was becoming less compliant. When we had arrived and checked in at the reception desk, we were told to have a seat. She said she would go and check at the nurses' station and pranced off blindly down the corridor. I waited a moment, then followed her at a distance. At the nurses' station she was told that it was early yet, so we sat in the inner waiting room. She turned to me and said, "You could go home ahead of me and I'll join you as soon as I'm finished," as though she were perfectly self-sufficient and she could leave the building, hail a cab, and go home. She not only wanted to continue to live: she wanted her independence back and at that instant I was standing in the way of it.

I called Hare to let him know we would be late. When I returned to the waiting room, there was a large bloodstain on the chair where the Princess had been sitting and a trail of blood on the carpet in the hallway and all the way to the bathroom. I thought it was a good thing she couldn't see very well. The nurse was clearly overwhelmed. She came with a container of spray cleaner and a little rag and wiped the stains off the linoleum and the carpet. She dropped a chuck, a sheet of blue plastic lined with quilted white tissue, onto the stained seat. Then she went to the bathroom to help the Princess wash and give her some fresh pads. When the Princess returned to sit on the blue plastic pad I noticed that she had blood on one hand and I fetched a paper towel, ran it under a tap and rubbed off the blood—painstakingly, for it had dried. The only possible blood on her hands was the guilt of omission: it was by way of an unwitting apology, perhaps, that she had contracted the same illness her daughter had died of. She who had never allowed her family to invade her let illness do so now.

That afternoon, for the first time, the lilac-haired doctor suggested he and I fetch the Princess at the radiation table: it must have been an ordeal. Her head was towards the door. She lay on the table, her knees bent, her beautiful young girl's legs elegantly stretched out on the crinkly vellum. Three attendants were strapping what looked like a giant diaper between her legs. "She is like our mother," the doctor told me. "She knows we like her." The Princess descended from the table and he took her gently by the arm. I walked on the other side of her. He whispered to her, "We put lead to shield the rectum." When he left, she said, "I protest, this is too much. I am never coming here again, not for a visit nor for radiation." The doctor asked to check her again a week later.

After a night at the castle, breakfast beneath the greeny glow of a fluorescent sculpture. The Princess tottered in, shaky in her white wool dressing gown with white satin piping, the nightgown just protruding from beneath the hem on one side, and at the neck, her ever-present blue cashmere cardigan. She wore no makeup and I found she looked more beautiful so, strangely younger, her hair straight but uncombed yet. When she wore makeup, often applying too much of it, there was a painted look to her. I went up to her and kissed her on both cheeks, feeling what I always felt whenever I did so—that there was little to hug as her body recoiled from effusions and one was left with a handful of unyielding bones.

She walked on uncertain feet clad in faded red espadrilles around the kitchen, as though to will her blood to circulate, and went to the stove to turn the flame on under the coffee-pot. She had known a writer, she said, who made himself coffee every morning, then fed his pet turtle a leaf of lettuce. He had looked up the word *turtle* in his encyclopedia and found "animal endowed with scanty intelligence," which he liked to repeat. She thought of Giorgio Bassani, another writer she had known very well but hadn't seen for a long time—she enumerated all the literary prizes at which he had not been present. Hare said, "I thought he died." "Died?" The Princess was startled. "Why should he have died?"

After a pause, Hare said, "He must have been well over seventy. . . ."

I turned to my side of the bed and closed my eyes. Hare came to lie next to me, put his arm around my waist, his hand on my stomach, and I went back to sleep. Later, I heard him take a bath, flipping the water from the tub onto his hair to rinse it, and he came out wearing a towel around his waist smelling of soap and warm washed skin. I washed, splashing ice-cold water from the single tap by the tub onto myself, my eyes on the laundry hamper of ancient discolored plastic and woven rattan by the sink that had been there as long as I had gone to the castle.

On the mantelpiece, I noticed that my picture had been removed for Maro's recent visit, though one of her was there; a flannel nightgown hung on a hook, and a faded rose sweater of hers lay upside down as though it had just been removed on another hamper—these signs of her passing and familiarity with the place disturbed me as they always did. I saw a photo album on one of the shelves with a sprig slipped in between a plastic wrap and the cover. I knew instantly it must be a family album Maro had put together for Hare. When he was not looking, I peeked and saw a picture of Ruy, looking very young, holding a blond baby, no doubt Moon. Pictures exclude the sound and smell of children, of families as a whole, and their animal needs— the feeding, excrement, sleep, lack of sleep, the battle of wills. There is not a single picture in the world of the arguments that punctuate a marriage. Snapshots are never taken in moments of anger and therefore pictures are nearly always partial. They might capture something surreptitiously there, but not violent outbursts, incomprehension, isolation, boredom, the feeling of wanting to be elsewhere, unlove, or the amount of time situations last. The adult subjects of family pictures usually want to be remembered and to remember themselves in a good light, want a souvenir of goodness, of beauty and happiness, not of strife. And so the myth of family is perpetuated through pictures of families in their good moments. Children given birth to, raised, then they themselves making children, raising them, as generation after generation is duped by the apparent glories of family into perpetuating the family while the rows, the aggressions, the chronic torments are forgotten, buried with those who lived through them and kept them secret so as not to lose face. But would I have the strength to look through the entire album? Jealousy's imaginings are as conventional as any snapshot.

His voice sounded husky and she wondered how he could have such stores of grief—where they began and whether they could ever end. She wondered whether he would always be so and decided quietly she would stay by him no matter.

He returned to the same place in his brain cyclically, to the subject of her betrayal, and asked all the questions again as he had done then, as though she had not answered them all before as best as she could with the scalpel plunged deep into her entrails. She knew when the inquisition was coming because it was preceded by an unexpected outburst of rage.

Why had she deceived him? Out of a sense of duty. She had been offered marriage, a house, the quiet to work without worrying about rent—and children. She should have known they were too many things. Also that if she didn't already have them it was because she had not wanted them. Still, she felt she should want them—she, too, after all, was the prisoner of a dream, the dream of marriage. The spell of wanting a "normal" life, someone else's, what she had seen others doing with theirs, what every Jane Austen heroine did to make a book end happily. The dream of happiness can destroy every possibility of "happiness," those flickers of light cast over the fold of an afternoon, so fleeting that they could later be disbelieved or forgotten, so slight that they could pass unnoticed.

And Hare had not forgiven, would never do so. But she had suffered horribly. She had not been taught to refuse a man's wishes. Unmoving lips—she should have known then and run away. What kept her there? Awkwardness. The muffled heat. The little wooden house buried in damp tropical jungle. The silence. The immediate offer: come live here with me. The spell of those words. She fell for the invitation and whatever in her had elicited it. But what of the spirit who recognized only Hare? It fled.

For days it was lost and every time she returned to that muffled house she no longer knew who she was, ate things she did not like, had conversations she did not care to have, slept with a person she did not know, awoke inside a body that was the only familiar place in that entire landscape of mistaken adventure. Her spirit fled, which showed how unstable identity was. But how could she prove this to Hare? How could she prove to him that she had not been away from him a single instant? She beat and shouted the strange current away, and one day there was so much of her back that she was able to tell the stranger she never wanted to see him again, not to call. After all, she had no idea who it was that had spent some days with him. Her visit to hell smelt of the tropics, was filled with the inability to move, the ability to go against herself, poisoning all that was sweet in her life for the sake of a standard dream. Her visit to hell was to know the universe and every man and woman in it benevolent compared to her, to her murdering ways. She was a liar and a conformist who had found she could be her own best hell, the prisoner of a dream that had come

close to killing her. And at last, she was able to divorce her-
self from it.

I let her eye fall on a fable from the Panchatantra, *and she*
liked it so much she read it to him. A holy man transforms a
mouse into a little girl and brings her to his wife, since they
have no children. The little girl is wonderful and they
become very fond of her. When she turns twelve, her father
feels he must find her a husband. He brings her the sun, but
the girl finds him too hot. The sun says, "A cloud is supe-
rior to me because behind it I vanish." The father brings his
daughter a cloud, but she finds him too drifty and frigid.
What is superior to a cloud? the father asks. The cloud
replies, "The wind, for it can blow me away." So he brings
his daughter the wind, but she finds him too shifty. What is
superior to the wind? The wind replies, "The mountain,
because it stays still though I may blow with all my might."
The father brings his daughter the mountain, but she finds
him too stiff and rough. What is greater than a mountain?
The mountain says, "A mouse." He brings her a mouse and
she begs the holy man, her father, to turn her into a mouse
so that she may keep house for her husband the mouse. It is
done.

The moral of the tale: If one is a mouse, one will only be
happy in the company of mice. She is like the mouse who
was transformed into a little girl, only to discover that she
was a mouse through and through. She wakes up happy
that he is there, touches his arm, caresses his temple, and
knows it.

Hare had just acquired a painting of a man with his heart

being nibbled on either side by a white mouse and a black mouse. In exchange for it, he gave the artist a tall wooden bird from Senafu, in western Africa, that had an immense bill growing downwards into its neck, like a looping over-cooked asparagus stalk.

W hat has happened to me?" the Princess asked. "Who ever thought I would have to bear so much? I took the idea of radiations lightly. I thought it would be nothing." We had gone upstairs because after my walk in the snow my feet were frozen and didn't seem to want to warm up, though I was wearing stockings and long woollen argyle socks. In her bedroom, I sat by the window, in front of the ancient stove, beneath a painting of ducks with pink down feathers pasted on them and wrapped in thick transparent vinyl. The Princess reclined on a futon laid on a wooden frame, the backrest tilted up. She had her transparent *fumé* stockings—no matter how cold it was, she never wore slippers or wool tights—her blue jersey Givenchy dress with a green trim, and the green sweater with gold buttons. It was extraordinary how new her clothes looked given the amount of wear they received.

The storm had fizzled, only the icy cold remained. There was such sweetness in her sometimes when I saw her alone: she could be calm, simple, undemanding, solicitous. This was what always attracted me to her. I remembered her shyness.

How would it be not to have to see oneself every day? I dreamt of vanishing into a state of being from which to observe the world and not be observed. Maintenance of the body is one of the true drudgeries of life. No sooner is it done than it must be redone.

As we were watching television, after a dinner of white rice, peas, scrambled eggs, and ice cream, the phone rang, and it was Hare. The Princess spoke to him first and I ascertained from her reaction that he would not return that evening but the following afternoon, Sunday. She handed me the receiver, and he said, "I do not want the Princess to know, but I had a little accident—I cut my head and had to have thirty-five stitches." "Your head, again," I said, remembering the time before, boarding a Pakistani airline flight, when he had cut his head on the trunk of a taxi. He had splashed it with bourbon so as not to get an infection, then had reclined in his seat in all his alcoholic fragrance surrounded by Muslims staring at him suspiciously. Then there was the time when a thatched roof had collapsed on him on a remote Mexican beach; he had been there with his family.

As I took the phone, the Princess whispered to me, "You could sleep here anyway, couldn't you?" Hare thought I should, since I had come with the idea of doing so. A few days earlier, Maro had slept alone in his bed, now I would do so. It had never happened in the decade I had known Hare, and it felt odd. I listened for noises, whisperings in the walls, sighings at the windows, the squeaking drone of the elevator from the house next door. The Princess always said that there were suspicious noises in every room in the house, and she blamed it on the presence of spirits inhabiting the tribal sculptures.

Before I undressed to go to bed, I picked up the photo album from the shelf, sat on the edge of the bed and went through it three times, turning the pages very slowly, observing every picture: Hare with his first child, Hare in an air-port, holding the little blond child by one hand, pulling him up so his feet were off the ground, Hare looking thin in blue corduroy pants, light jacket, blue sweater, his straight black hair, intense, delicate face, the eyes larger and darker than now. Hare at dinners—one in the garden of the castle with three artists: Jean-Michel Basquiat, Francesco Clemente, and Andy Warhol. Hare with his second baby. The second baby with her mother, looking blond, sweet, exhausted, and rather happy. Hare holding the baby, sitting back in a chair and yawning. At the end, just slipped in, was a photo of Maro when she was younger, her face slim, her features regular, her nose small, blond hair cut short and layered, making her look boyish; she wore a shirt and over it a white Mexican jumper in thick wool with little embroideries at the sleeves and neckline and a colored cord to tie at the neck—all the hope was there, the innocence of a woman starting a family. As the album progressed, a strange satisfaction seeped through the dissatisfaction. Every now and then, a picture of her smiling, and kindness was there. She was always near Hare, never letting him go, even in a recent note to him on the table, with the collage of a heart on it, she used language I sometimes heard on him; words like *relax* and *tension,* and *wonderful* and *love,* and *look at the plans for fixing the house.* All the banal assurances I furnished myself as to why he was with me dissipated: I was not better, only differ-ent. Or: whatever kept us together was nothing you could put your finger on, nothing obvious.

The curtains collapsing off the hooks in the bedroom, the couple in the canvas on the mantelpiece dancing with their heads in a bubble—true of any couple. I listened to the little noises in the walls, my own life so quiet. I lit a small light on the table that illumined a terra-cotta figure with its hands in its disheveled curls and went to sleep thinking of it and me.

In the morning, the Princess came down as soon as she heard me and finished off the coffee she had made for herself earlier. She was already dressed. When I left, she said, "Come back soon. It's civil death here without you."

Days later, I found the Princess on the flowery couch. I took out a little radio I had bought for her, put in some batteries, found a good channel, set it on the couch. She didn't touch or look at it, as though I had introduced an unwelcome presence between us. She said, "I don't know how to use those things." I could feel her antagonism. She began to complain that Hare was leaving again, that it might not be a good thing for his head wound, that he was always leaving. She was saying, in between the words, that she wished we were not going. She was bitter today, hiding none of her displeasure.

I said, "If you don't want this radio, I'll return it. You don't seem to care for it." She said, "Yes, please do. I already have two of them in Rome I never listen to." I packed the radio up in its box and in a suppressed fury went downstairs, conscious only of the desire to get away from her. I pretended to read a book in the hallway. Hare came down, found me there, asked if something was amiss. I said I had no one but myself to blame: the Princess did not like gifts, and she did not like radios, that much was clear. I had sworn I would not give her any more gifts, but I had forgotten. I had done so out of a vague sense of guilt that we were both leaving her for a week, though she would have Lupe to take care of her, a friend to take her to the doctor, a nephew to come and see her, someone else to take her to a gallery. But she no longer liked being alone, even for an afternoon.

In the hallway, I thought how ungrateful it was of her to begrudge me a week with Hare. I went to sit around the table of jackets and books and read articles strewn on it, but distractedly, my mind still on my rage. Hare went to grill some steaks, she came to sit by me and attempted to make conversation. Why had such an artist not been mentioned in a paper? What a provincial paper, how ignorant they were. How old so-and-so looked in a photograph, didn't I think so? I said none of it mattered very much. My seething continued through the first part of lunch. Hare's face was very much worse, his left eye so swollen it had narrowed to a slit, and it was red and purple so that he had to wear sunglasses. But his mood was calm.

Yesterday, while we were still in bed, he said that the fall should have been a quiet time for him, a time when he should have been alone to make sense of things, and instead the Princess had become the center of everything, in a way delaying his separation from Maro just by being there. The Princess was keeping us all in our places.

On Sundays Lupe never left the basement, so the Princess set the table, with modesty and an economy of movements, then swept the dirty pans and dishes into the dishwasher.

Suddenly she was leaving. A nephew who had come for a conference had offered to accompany her back to Rome.

Suddenly, after all the wanting to leave of the previous months, she didn't want to go. She began, as Hare did, too, when on the brink of losing something, to regret it, forgetting any pain it might have caused. They hated to lose anything that had once been theirs, as though the fact alone of it having belonged to them conferred on it inestimable value.

There were four hundred horses at the estate in the country where she had been raised with her brother, by the bailiff and his wife. "Our parents were blissfully absent," she told me, not for the first time, "and when we saw them, they were distant." The horses came to drink every day at sundown, and when the mean bull came to drink, the children were made to go indoors. The spell that the Princess cast had been diminished by the number of times her tales had been told. The quips and anecdotes had become refrains: "Stupidity gives you a sense of the infinite," or, "They say that in Moscow a rope was stretched from one end of the city to the other . . ." (which was a line of dialogue from Chekhov's *Three Sisters*). Her excellent memory for the thoughts of others was so vivid that for a long time one was persuaded that they were hers when in fact she was their secretary, their official rememberer. When she knew you knew, she stopped, ran dry, stopped noticing you, stopped trying to entertain you.

Her memories . . . She had seen polo played for the first time in England by three maharajahs in all their raiment: she remembered their speed, precision, deftness, the frequency with which the horses were changed—after that, she had lost all desire to watch anyone else playing the game, as it would never again be such a wondrous spectacle. There it was again, the exclusivity—polo played by maharajahs or not at all; Hamlet impersonated by Gielgud or no one; Shakespeare and Leopardi or nothing. Of course she, her family, those closest to her all belonged, invisibly, to the "nothing" category. She revered only artists and thought of them constantly, tried to inhabit their brains, even when she did not like their work.

She had lived most of her married life surrounded by painters, illustrators, writers, poets, most of whom never became known beyond the confines of Italy, much to her dismay. They made wonderful companions. The Princess was entertained by them and no doubt entertained them, too. She did not even have a high school degree because she had failed a math exam and had never gotten around to retaking it. The following years she had attended lectures at the university but never sat for the exams. She didn't think it was worth it, either because it had all been done before, or because one should not even attempt anything unless one had been born a genius.

At lunch Hare, a nephew, and the Princess were saying, "Yes, that was the greatest contribution of the West . . ." They all agreed. I had missed what had been the greatest contribution of the West and later had to ask Hare. He said, "Habeas corpus, 'you have the body,' to release an individual from unlawful imprisonment." The law touched on whether a prisoner had been accorded due process rather than on establishing guilt or innocence. "In the East this does not even begin to exist," the Princess murmured, latching on to one of her favorite occupations—denigrating the universe with the exception of the world she knew. Then she sang under her breath, " 'I am prisoner of a dream, prisoner of a dream that will be the death of me . . .' "

She sat, on her last night at the castle before her return to Rome, wearing a white satin blouse with large buttons, a black cardigan, her pearls, a grey skirt, and she sat as always beneath the painted crucified feet and the brown squiggled painting. She smoked, drank a shot of scotch. When I had gone upstairs after making dinner, she had not even greeted me. I no longer existed because now I was part of the family. It was what she was accused, by some, of doing with her own children: they were expected to be there, "as ornaments," Hare had said.

Habeas corpus—she had her body, and she took it with her to Rome.

The last time the Princess and I went to the park, one Saturday afternoon, it was a sunny day, and warm. There were sudden gusts of wind from different directions. We watched the dense carpet of russet leaves being blown east, settling back on the ground, then being blown west. There were little white clouds moving slowly, a turquoise sky with red in it.

The Princess cited the 1571 battle of Lepanto, the first major Ottoman defeat by Christian powers, ending the myth of Ottoman naval invincibility, and the single factor that had brought Islamic supremacy to an end.

At the airport, the sun was setting. I took a picture of her and she said, "I don't like photographs, in fact, I detest them." She refused to let me carry the black canvas bag into which she had put the bronze the sculptor had given her. She almost refused to let Hare carry it for her, but he took it from her hands, and she could hardly protest. All her apparent lack of interest in possessions proved to be another mask: she would let no one take what was hers. She had accepted the gift with grace and not even a hint of surprise or exaggerated gratitude—like the true Princess she was. The fierceness with which she guarded her treasure now was a revelation. Her style was to always pretend not to want, not to need, not to suffer, not to feel—only to think, to reason, to reduce the world to intelligence. But with the bronze all that fell away. She asked me what she could give the sculptor in exchange for his gift. I said I did not think there was anything other than a letter but Hare found a large book on Michelangelo for her to give. Even when she had indeed been moved, she found it hard to *give* anything, other than her time and tales. She had given me those unstintingly day after day, and I had taken them and committed her to memory—the Princess stilled in portrait.

I accompanied her to the bathroom twice. The last radiation had had this effect. Hare told her the doctor said nothing needed to be done now, for the time being. "What does it mean, 'for the time being'?" she asked alarmed. "I hoped after six months to have a cure." But the doctor did not speak of cures: the radiation had greatly reduced but not eliminated the tumor. There was every possibility that it would return, but perhaps he speculated that it would not return for some time, and the Princess was already eighty-nine.

The orange setting sun shone on her face, made the gold buttons on her grey dress sparkle and brightened the green braiding at the collar and down the front. "Where is my bag?" she asked. It was on a seat in front of her. There were no tears when the time came for her to engage the corridor leading to the door of the plane. Moments earlier she had said to me, "Those were beautiful moments yesterday at the park." That was all. She had been more explicitly affectionate to Lupe, knowing that Lupe would not understand the brand of restraint reserved for members of the family. So to her she said, *"Te quiero molto,"* which means "I love you," in a combination of Spanish and Italian, then added, "really."

At the first dinner after the going of the Princess, her love, the sculptor, came. He sat at the head of the table and showed a young woman he had come with how to tie a hangman's noose, twisting the string seven times around itself and widening the loop to demonstrate how it could be made to accommodate a head, then be drawn tight around the neck.

Hare brought an African object from upstairs: a figure of a man, standing bullishly as though bearing a tremendous weight, with ropes tied around the shoulders and neck, and over his head a mask of a snarling animal similar to a crocodile, with long jaws and sharp fangs. "Could it have been a toy?" the sculptor asked. "A toy?" the African artist who had done the napkin dance with the Princess asked. *"This?"* It was, he said, the fetish of a dancer and used for sacrifices. The patina had been given by the blood of animals—chickens, sheep, goats.

The sculptor's wife had gone away, taking her child with her. She would not return. "What does he see in her?" the Princess had muttered days before leaving, as any jealous lover would.

In the dream, his house is a castle enveloped in darkness. He may be in it somewhere, but I never know in which room. I make my way in the dark, careful not to wake Maro who may be asleep in the room with Hare, beneath a painted green field. Sometimes she is not there at all, but I have no way of knowing. I creep down long corridors, into unlit rooms, my arms outstretched to feel for the form of a bed. When I find it, I lie down hoping no one will surprise me in it. I lie awake listening to noises in the house. I hear steps. At times I am certain that they are his steps and long to call out, but that I must not do. Once or twice Maro awakes, comes into the room. I hear her breathing. I am certain she will walk over to my bed, but before she has a chance to, I tiptoe out of the room, down the stairs, out of the house, across the garden, into the fields, into the night, so she will not find me. Once she materialized in the middle of a very grand affair in the garden to which I had been invited. The castle was even larger that time. There were many separate wings and tall glass doors to the terrace so that one could enter and leave unseen or suddenly come face-to-face with someone one had not known was there. I dreamt of the castle again while asleep in his house. He had been working upstairs, woke me when he came to bed and that is how I knew I had been dreaming.

I dreamt I went to Hare's house and Maro was there. It

was not the Gloomy Castle but a place in the country. Several guests had preceded me. Maro looked wan, there were lines around her eyes. She looked at me tenderly, took my hands in between hers and murmured, "At last we meet." It was as though she had long awaited this moment. To her left two men in dark suits laughed urbanely. I went up to the first, giving him my hand, but he drew close and kissed me on the mouth, then spurted saliva through my lips. I couldn't quite decide whether it was an accident, but when the second man did the same thing, I knew it was a conspiracy. They were taking revenge for my treatment of Maro whereas Maro herself seemed unperturbed. I can remember little else, save that there had been a long ivory necklace made of skulls I had dropped on a lawn and that I thought towards the end of the dream how complicated it would be to get it back, to describe the object and the circumstances of its disappearance.

"Were you ever arrested, Bing?" a film character played by Tony Curtis asked his butler. "Only once, sir," the man replied, bowing slightly, "for bigamy."

I forget now all the talk of the perfection of triangles.

Since they, Maro, the Princess—the "other women"—have gone, it's been a *honeymoon*.

The father of the Princess was more or less forced into marrying a young woman his family had chosen for him and when the match failed very early on, he resorted to brothels though his wife was very beautiful. In fact, the Princess overheard her schoolmates say once, "Her mother is more beautiful than she is," and the Princess had been very proud of that as children can be of their parents.

The mother was a moralist and could be obsessive. The Princess had inherited from her the way she had of fixating on a subject: "She becomes obtuse when she is like that, and that's when I lose my temper," said Hare. Her parents' marriage was grim, and the Princess had suffered its effects. Hare suggested, "You should ask the Princess about it, she would talk to you. I know fragments only." But the Princess would not speak to me of such things: she did not approve of giving herself away except where it might paint an image of amusement, beauty, wit, above all lightness. The detrimental, the miserly, niggardly, harrowing were outside her range of vision; not so tragedy, which she saw clearly without deception or false hope, and it was this greatness in her that could so mislead one to continue down the shadowy path to her heart where one was met with the fall of the axe, delivered by an automated system no one, least of all she, controlled; simply to draw near was to activate it.

Hare's father confessed to his son that he would still choose in a wife the combination of extreme intelligence and charm coupled with a certain detachment over a more demonstrative woman. What did he know of affection? His own mother had died when he was a child. At the age of thirty, by himself in London and suffering from acute depression, due in part to the political situation in Italy (the murder of Matteotti), he had converted to Catholicism. He suffered from insomnia and his father, a neurologist, told him, "Then don't sleep," discouraging him from taking sleeping pills.

He went to mass every Sunday but did not force anyone else in the family to do so. Hare said that the Princess was so Catholic she didn't even need to go to mass but generally avoided the clergy.

As a girl, she had played with her brother and a friend, a member of the papal nobility, enacting mock masses. Their other favorite game was the cat corrida: they would tie a little tin pan to the cat's tail, then let him run down a long corridor making a rattling racket of cymbals. They would jump out from side doorways and block his passage as if he were a bull, brandishing a stick and yelling, "¡Aja, Toro!"

The Princess's sudden rages stopped after her husband died. She had had fits of rage against her own mother. Hare adopted a system to put a stop to the Princess's meandering diatribes.

A perfect day. We had dinner at an Indian restaurant. It drizzled but not enough for us to want to be indoors: Hare observed, after a woman walked by in a funny mincing step, her thighs pressed together, that certain walks reminded him of nature programs—he thought she walked like a deer.

We ordered something "very good, too difficult to explain," as the waiter said, and lamb vindaloo. The evening reminded us of one July Fourth weekend when we talked until the early hours of the morning sitting at a sidewalk café, long past the hour of closing. When I had gone home that night, I didn't think I would see him again.

We watched TV, went to bed, woke up, made love, fell asleep, made love, and there were little drops of blood on the eiderdown, the top sheet, the bottom sheet, the mattress. I dragged it all to the bathroom to wash it, leaving Hare on a bare mattress till he went downstairs to the pantry to bring up three large plastic containers of detergent, spot remover, bleach. They were magic, as commercials always say they are. All I had to do was rub a little blue liquid and the stains came out. But still, there was a lot of rubbing, rinsing, then draping everything to dry over doors and lamps and wherever I could find room. I relished this nocturnal laundering, told Hare it reminded me just how tedious it was to wash clothes but also how satisfying to have a task that could be started and finished in a matter of minutes. On the mattress, covered only with a brown and straw-colored Mexican blanket, Hare folded one leg at the knee like a yogi. Somewhere between one submersion into him and another I looked at his face and wanted to be beneath his skin, felt I was.

It was past one in the afternoon and we hadn't even had breakfast. At the boathouse, sparrows gathered on the rope in front of us and waited for crumbs. I kept Hare's raincoat and black beret on though there was a white tent above our heads: a heron, later a duck; the reflection of turquoise boats and brown trunks, the haze of green leaves in the water. Hare looked happy.

The painter made a black-and-white portrait of him: his eyes were very large like coal mines; the furrow in his brow was just the way it was, but then the nose is small, the face short—it may not have looked like Hare except for something in the eyes, but it was him, as though a part of him inhabited the picture.

The Princess's voice from Rome on my answering machine had the slightest crack in it, a new weariness I had never heard in it before. The illness of the past fortnight and its cures—antibiotics, painkillers—and the news that the cancer had once again crept its way back had aged her. Or perhaps it was age that had aged her: in a month she would be ninety.

She was in a clinic in Rome, a few doors down from where the pope had been hospitalized days before. She had a cystoscopy: a tube was inserted to bypass the clogged urethra. Though the operation had gone well and the Princess seemed to be recovering, she was unable to keep any food down: she tried to eat a little but immediately got the hiccups. The only nourishment she was receiving was intravenous. The oncologist noted a "pelvic recidiva with an infiltration to the bladder." The cancer was spreading.

The Princess—not her mind, but her body—may have secretly given up, decided it was time to stop being brave, time to stop thinking life continued to hold any promise, if only the promise of itself with its quiet unfolding, its measured surprises, the greatest one being its livability beyond the notion of a future, the day-by-day existence she led, taking an interest in her world and in the world at large, its politics, its culture, its minute detail, its grandeur. She, the Princess, was at the center of a universe still ruled by reason, her enlightened universe on the brink of extinction, a brink between her own life and death. Some of the greatness of her world was poised to vanish with her. But she could still have found the resolve to return. Perhaps if Hare went to Italy to see her . . . He too lived day by day now, ready to change his plans at a moment's notice. He was thinking of her now, at the back of his mind, hour by hour. He showed someone a photograph of her the sculptor had taken the summer before. She wore a white piqué suit, the jacket loosely belted and left slightly open over a dark navy shirt, standing next to the sculptor looking glamorous, poised, on the brink—happy.

I can still see her sitting in one of the armchairs in her bedroom in Rome. The armrests are worn down where hands have rested again and again and for long spells over the decades: there are deep elliptical wounds in the pale yellow fabric and they reveal the layers of upholstery—burlap, horsehair—and finally the very core shrouding the wooden frame and the void within. Her younger son found little pieces of the same fabric, perhaps from some concealed part of the covers, and placed them over the gaping holes, then pinned them in place with white plastic dome-headed pins stuck right through the different layers. She, too, like the furniture, was worn down to her core: she was in a white cotton honeycomb dressing gown, the sack of her recent colonoscopy and long tubes emerging from beneath the hem, sitting hunched forward, the hands clutching the wounded armrests, her hair lanky and uncut and falling down the sides of her face. It hadn't grown much, considering it had been months since she had been to the hairdresser, but the two inches it had grown gave her a wild appearance so unlike her former self. That, and the fact she was no longer wearing her elegant uniforms, or any makeup. She no longer even had the strength to wear the face of "herself." She was stranded on the wreck of her own body and she herself only barely alive on the only plank left which was beginning to give way.

Why could she not have had a hysterectomy instead of all

the radiation that had finally brought her to this extreme physical decline? Had the doctors underestimated her strength at the second onset of cancer? She had been eighty-seven then but she could have withstood a long operation better than all the gradual and finally lethal "treatments." She and we had all been prisoners of a dream—that the doctors would "cure" her. She herself had been the greatest believer. And because doctors, even oncologists, prefer to speak of cures, favoring the slim chance of success—their bedside manner—they let their patients in for a long routine that kills slowly, the body as well as hope itself. They cured their patients of illusion, if nothing else. Cured them of the desire to go on living, of any remaining ability to do so. They prepared them for a death feared from the very first diagnosis of cancer and later rendered certain, after a number of treatments, when the body proved unwilling to comply with the more optimistic prognostications: that the radiation would kill only harmful cells without harming healthy ones.

There was no way to be of any use to the Princess, no saving her from the cure.

I had been so close to her, I no longer had any illusions about her—it was the way I felt about myself: I had become her, a story at a time. She was dying, I remained. Or we were both dying, and we both lived, since she had poured herself into me. So I worried, for both of us, about the present. Christmas. What to make for lunch. The small world of day-to-dayness. Her world—that of her body only, for her mind was in mine and that of all who remembered her—was dwindling.

With the third bout of fever caused by an infection of the artificial urine ducts, a final injection of morphine was administered. Still, two days before she died, speaking to me on the telephone, she remembered the seven different theatre productions she had seen of *Hamlet,* all played by Gielgud. "He was different each time," she said; "he tried to improve, to simplify, to reach the essential." It might have been a description of herself as she presented herself to the outside world. She had told me once, "If something I read or look at depresses me, I say to myself, 'This is not art.' For that is the sign of true art—if it lifts you out of your gloom. But artists now paint the void since we are probably living in one. Still, that is no reason to paint it."

The Princess in her ninetieth year.

Christmas: Hare brought her a Nativity scene inside of a coconut painted bright green—the Madonna, a pink-faced wormlike creature with black rays emanating from her head; a pink black-haired baby Jesus with feet like the fins of a fish; it came with a postcard of a hand-painted ESSO sign hanging from a tree on the back of which Hare had written, "Aquerò," the word Bernadette read in an appari-

tion of the Virgin Mary, "It is!" I continue the list of gifts: a pig-faced angel blowing into a trumpet; a naked yellow dancing nymph with three black buns on her head (like Popeye's Olive Oyl) and pursed red lips; a wooden spoon with spikes for spaghetti; a watercolor of a forlorn lion; a pale terra-cotta woman with her chin thrust forward, a long nose, large breasts, wide hips, and a big round belly, tall as the palm of one hand; a little silver box with a squat spherical body such as a djinn might hide in, between lives. On it was my motto, "Fall away my body of worry."

Gini Alhadeff was born in Alexandria, Egypt. She is the author of a memoir, *The Sun at Midday.*